LOVE WILL FIND YOU

The Knights of Berwyck, A Quest Through Time

SHERRY EWING

Copyright © 2020 by Sherry Ewing

All rights reserved.

No part of this book may be reproduced in any form or by any electronic or mechanical means, including information storage and retrieval systems, without written permission from the author, except for the use of brief quotations in a book reviews.

Kingsburg Pres
P.O. Box 475146
San Francisco, CA 94147
www.kingsburgpress.com

Love Will Find You is a work of fiction. Names, characters, places, and incidents are a product of the author's imagination. Locales and public names are sometimes used for atmospheric purposes. Any resemblance to actual people, living or dead, or to businesses, companies, events, institutions, or locales is completely coincidental.

Editor: Jude Knight
Front Cover Design:
www.SelfPubBookCovers.com/ INeedABookCover
Back Cover Design: by Sherry Ewing

Love Will Find You/Sherry Ewing -- 1st ed.
ISBN eBook: 978-1-946177-51-3
ISBN Print: 978-1-946177-52-0
Library of Congress Control Number: 2019905629

OTHER BOOKS BY SHERRY EWING

Medieval & Time Travel Series

*To Love A Scottish Laird: De Wolfe Pack
Connected World*

*To Love An English Knight: De Wolfe Pack
Connected World*

If My Heart Could See You: The MacLaren's

For All of Ever: The Knights of Berwyck,
A Quest Through Time (Book One)

Only For You: The Knights of Berwyck,
A Quest Through Time (Book Two)

Hearts Across Time: The Knights of Berwyck,
A Quest Through Time (Books One & Two)
A special box set of For All of Ever & Only For You

A Knight To Call My Own: The MacLaren's

To Follow My Heart: The Knights of Berwyck,
A Quest Through Time (Book Three)

The Piper's Lady within *Never Too Late:* A Bluestocking Belles
Collection 2017

Love Will Find You: The Knights of Berwyck,
A Quest Through Time (Book Four)

One Last Kiss: The Knights of Berwyck,
A Quest Through Time (Book Five)

Regency's

A Kiss for Charity: *A de Courtenay Novella (Book One)*

The Earl Takes A Wife: *A de Courtenay Novella (Book Two)*

Nothing But Time, *A Family of Worth: Book One*

One Moment In Time: *A Family of Worth, Book Two*

Under the Mistletoe

A Second Chance At Love in *Fire & Frost:* *A Bluestocking Belles Collection*

Join Sherry's newsletter at http://bit.ly/2vGrqQM

www.SherryEwing.com

LOVE WILL FIND YOU

DEDICATION

For my dear friend Claudia

We may not have known each other long but you've become a sister of my heart. Thank you for the beautiful covers you've designed for me but more importantly your friendship. Continue to fight the fight. You're a strong woman and I know you've got this.

Love Will Find You *is for you, Claudia.*
May you find a new adventure to fill your soul between these pages!

PART I
A SECOND TIME FOR LOVE

CHAPTER 1

Beach near Berwyck Castle
The Year of Our Lord's Grace 1182

Ella Fitzpatrick was weary to the bone. With her shoes dangling from her fingertips, she trudged her way across the strand at a slow pace. The cold ocean waters stung her sore feet as the waves rushed up to her ankles. She barely noticed the pain for she was at least content to be near the vast sea once more. The sound of the ocean always calmed her, as much as was possible given that her thoughts left her constantly on edge.

She was tired of wandering from place to place. Tired of trying to keep her mind from straying to what could be... or had been. Tired of keeping one step ahead of her relentless pursuer. Tired of always remembering to speak as though she belonged here. Tired of always struggling to do her best to keep herself grounded in the twelfth century rather than slipping back to her place of origin more than eight hundred years in the future.

Indeed, neither place in time was for her. Her mind shied away from the brothers and sisters, the nieces and nephews, left in Jacksonville, Florida, and from Simon of Hull, the husband she had consented to marry to anchor her in the twelfth century.

The peace fled from her entirely as she remembered what happened after Simon died. What had she done to deserve her treatment? And why did her tormenter pursue her yet?

She drove back her despair. She had traveled through time to the place she belonged, then lost it – along with the man she loved. Returning to her true place and time had taken thirty years, living day after day, year after year. She was almost there.

Soon. Soon.

Her true love would ride where she first met him, and they would have a second chance. This time, she would not flee. This time…

The sound of thunder brought Ella out of her memories of her past life, or perchance 'twas her future life. Sometimes 'twas hard for her to tell which was which. She looked up. The clear sky showed no signs of rainfall. The beach began to vibrate beneath her, and she looked over her shoulder.

A small army galloped its way in her direction, impressive in their unison as they drove their steeds in a tight formation and at a brisk pace. Massive war horses as black as the midnight sky raced towards her. The knights were clothed also in black with the exception of their blood red capes billowing behind them in the ocean breeze. But recognition dawned quickly and Ella felt no fear, since Berwyck's standard flew proudly to identify the men.

The lead knight raised his arm, causing his men to halt their steeds. 'Twas clear they had but recently been in a battle given the condition of their clothes and the fresh cuts and slashes upon their bodies.

She made her way to the knight and his horse blew warm air from his nostrils as she came to pat his neck "Hello, Thor. You still carry your master well, do you not, my friend," she whispered with a fond smile. The horse nickered but Ella only laughed. "I am most sorry but I am afraid I have no treat for you this day."

"Ah, Lady Ella," Lord Dristan said with a welcoming smile. "A pleasure to see you once again."

"You have been in battle, my lord?" she asked, looking around the knights at signs of travail.

"A skirmish, no more," Lord Dristan replied. "A band of thieving rogues who thought to rob one of the villages we protect."

Any fools who thought to make a name for themselves by defeating the knight who had become the legendary Devil's Dragon of Berwyck probably deserved what they got, Ella thought. Her thirty years in this century had taught her hard lessons about the need for strong men to protect the weak.

Lord Dristan, the Devil's Dragon himself, was smiling in welcome. "I pray you shall be gracing Berwyck's halls for a time? 'Twill please my lady to see you again."

"Just Ella, my lord," she replied, "as I have told you many times in the past."

Dristan leaned forward to rest his arm upon the pommel of his saddle. "You must needs indulge my whims, my lady, for I see nothing but the fairest of ladies before me. Is this not so, Killian?"

Ella acknowledged the older knight next to Dristan's horse with a slight nod. Uncle to Dristan's lady, he was a handsome man as far as looks went. Tall with broad shoulders, his reddish-light brown hair with hints of grey hung just above his shoulders, his beard in need of a trim. She had spent a fair amount of time in his company these many years since she first found her way to the halls of Berwyck.

Killian had always been kind to her whenever they had idle conversation in the great hall, or within the lord and his lady's solar. She was momentarily startled by the appreciative look he gave her with his intense blue-green eyes. She had never noticed him looking upon her in such a fashion before this day.

"Aye, a lady in all ways, my laird," Killian declared while his gaze once again swept her from head to toe.

She felt herself blush, as any young maiden might have done from receiving the admiring glances of a handsome suitor. She must look a fright! How long it had been since she had found any form of comfort within a hall or inn, she could not say. Those knowing eyes of Killian's continued to hold her own, causing heat to rush to her flushed face.

She had never been vain about her appearance, but she did feel the compliment when Killian continued to assess her condition. It had been some time since a man had offered her any form of flattery and she was hard pressed to correct either of them in using the term *lady*. She did not care to be recognized as anything higher than what she considered herself. A common woman lost in time. No matter that circumstances were…

Dristan's merry chuckle brought her out of her musings. "We have left the fair woman speechless, it seems, Killian. Assist the lady so she may ride with you," he ordered.

"'Tis hardly necessary, my lord. Berwyck is close enough and the walk will do me good." Thor gave her a nudge with his nose, apparently still looking for something to eat. He almost knocked her over in his insistence she feed him. "Bad horse. I have nothing for you," she scolded wagging her finger at the animal.

"Behave, Thor." Dristan ordered while his steed tossed up his head, shaking his mane as though disappointed he would not receive a sweet. Dristan then grimaced when his gaze traveling to her abused feet. "You have walked far enough, if I were to guess, considering the state you are in, but 'tis of no matter. I insist you ride with us. We must make haste for we are in great need of sustenance to fill our bellies and quench our thirst. I refuse to allow a woman in our company to continue her travels without escort. See to her, Killian."

"Aye, my liege," Killian answered, dismounting from his horse as Dristan waved his arm and his men put their steeds into motion.

Yanking on the reins of his mount, Killian moved forward to stand before Ella. Looping the leather straps around the pommel, he offered her his assistance in order to mount the huge animal.

"May I, Lady Ella?" he inquired, holding out his hand to her.

She gave a weary sigh. There was no sense in attempting to remain indifferent to the orders he had been given. "If you must obey your lord, then I suppose I must too. But for heaven's sake, please call me Ella."

"'Tis not seemly ye should ask such of me, my lady."

Her brow rose at his obstinacy. 'Twas most irritating and she preferred to forget the part of her past that made such a statement true. "I must insist. I do not profess to be a lady of high rank and refuse to be treated as such. I am just Ella."

He turned his back on her momentarily, walking towards the ocean waves grumbling to himself about the stubbornness of some women. He returned with his decision. "If ye insist, then I must needs humor ye, I suppose. Let us away, Ella."

"A wise choice, Sir Killian."

"Just Killian," he replied, and his eyes twinkled in suppressed merriment, as if he expected her to resist dropping all formality between them.

With a small smile, she nodded her head. "Killian, then."

She took his outstretched hand and was briefly surprised when a tingle raced up her arm. He must have felt it too, because his eyes momentarily widened at their touch. He took her hand and placed it upon his shoulder as he in turn lifted her by her waist to place her upon his horse.

Once she was settled, Killian placed his foot in the stirrup and swung himself into the saddle. Since Ella was placed behind him, she made a fast grab for his waist when he flicked the reins and his horse bolted into motion. Her breath left her with his nearness and she swore she heard him give a chuckle.

They made their way quickly across the beach. Before long, Ella began to wonder what in the world had come over her while she felt her heart racing almost as fast as the horse lessened the distance to the castle growing ever nearer. She must be tired if being this close to a man who was not Henry was suddenly turning her emotions to mush.

Ella shook her head trying to clear her thoughts even as Killian took hold of her arms as though to hold her in place. She could not afford the distraction Killian would surely present. She would need to leave Berwyck as quickly as possible so as not to tempt fate more than she already had in her poor sorry life. She could not allow her pursuer to catch up with her. Her future with Henry was so close. He just did not know they were destined to meet yet.

CHAPTER 2

Killian watched Ella from afar as she made her way across the great hall to her place next to Lady Amiria on the raised dais. He had always found her a handsome woman. Her brown hair was pulled back away from her face in a long thick braid; he pondered how she would look with the locks tumbling into place down her back. 'Twas not the first time he had such thoughts for they reoccurred each time she wandered her way to Berwyck. He wished to be the man to release those very same tresses from their confinement, and not the phantom man of whom she had spoken of to Amiria's friend Katherine. He hated that she was waiting for a man she had yet to meet to grant him such an honor.

He had been hard pressed to keep his mind where it belonged when she rode behind him on the way to the castle earlier this day. Taking one hand from the leather straps guiding his horse, he had taken delight in pulling her arms closer around him. He barely remembered muttering something about how he did not wish her to fall, not that he would ever let such happen to a woman left in his care.

Once reaching the stable, Killian had jumped from his horse and held out his arms to assist the lady from his steed. He rubbed his fingers together remembering how his hands had tingled when they wrapped around her waist. But Ella's feet had barely reached the ground before she was immediately whisked away to visit with Lady Amiria.

She had been closeted in Amiria's solar for what seemed like hours while Ella had speech with Lady Jenna, another one of those women from the future. They seemed to be showing up on a regular basis to fall in love with Berwyck's knights.

That had been several days ago. He had watched Ella from afar, keeping his heart where it belonged even while his mind pined away for her, as he did now, he in his place in the Great Hall, and she at the high table with Amiria. His mind continued roaming back to the first time he had seen Ella years ago, stumbling into the outer bailey with another woman as her companion. Killian was surprised to learn upon Lady Katherine's return to Berwyck that she had barely escaped her early demise from the evil plotting of her husband's ex-mistress. With Ella's help, she had fled back to Berwyck to seek shelter and from that time forward, Ella had traveled through its gates for many years.

This time, she and Killian had arrived together, but Killian was left feeling Ella's absence more than ever while his heart craved to be near her again. She seemed to be going out of her way to avoid him of late.

Ella looked up from her trencher and their gazes met. Did he but imagine her soft brown eyes widening when she noticed he had been staring at her or was this just his imagination running amuck? He nodded to her, raising his tankard in a silent toast before taking a sip and setting the mug back down upon the table. A slight smile rushed across her face before she returned her attention to her meal while her conversation with Lady Amiria resumed.

A sarcastic chuckle to his right caused Killian to ponder the knight next to him. Ulrick de Mohan swiped his sleeve across his lips.

Killian glared.

"What?" Ulrick muttered, trying to keep the smirk off his face but failing.

"Ye had something tae say tae me?" Killian all but growled, not wishing any jesting at his expense.

"You should go have speech with her," Ulrick replied. Of a sudden, he appeared serious. "You would not wish for someone else to occupy her time now, would you?"

"I do not know what ye are speaking about, lad." As Killian reached again for his ale, he noticed the table had grown eerily quiet.

"Lad?" Ulrick laughed. "I am no lad nor have I any notion of why you continue to consider us so. Have we not earned our spurs and proven our worth in the time we have defended these walls?" He gave Killian a nudge with his shoulder even as a chorus of *hear hear*s was accompanied by several of Dristan's personal guard slamming tankards upon the table in agreement.

"Mayhap we must needs prove our worth in the lists to the *old man...* again," Bertram, who was their captain, announced.

Killian frowned. "I am *not* so old that I still cannot best all of ye."

"Best listen to our elders, *lads*," Nathaniel called out. Laughter erupted from the knights.

Drake raised his chalice. "Plenty of daylight still. I accept the challenge."

"Nay! Not this eve," bellowed Turquine, as he gave a swat to the bottom of a pretty wench who refilled his tankard. "I have other more pleasurable ways to spend the night. The morn will come soon enough."

"I agree with my brother," Taegan added, "not that I have to prove myself. I, too, have plans to spend the eve with a woman who is sure to be kept busy 'til the early morn."

The men began hassling and jesting Taegan since all knew he had once favored a wench he thought was a virgin, yet the whole company had had a turn with her. Killian only cared the attention went to another. He did not wish to be ridiculed by his comrades in arms and all because of a woman he would never have.

The meal ended and the dishes were cleared while minstrels began playing for the lord and lady of the keep. Killian held out his tankard to be refilled. His mood had not improved with a full belly. Nor was drink going to change his disposition. He watched a member of the clan ask permission to dance with Ella. Dristan nodded his approval, along with the lady, and they moved to the center of the hall to begin the detailed patterns of the dance.

"You can still claim the Lady Ella," Ulrick said taking a sip of his drink. "'Tis not too late."

"Ye are wrong on that account," Killian answered beneath his breath before a heavy sigh of defeat left him unexpectedly.

"'Tis plain to see you favor her."

"I said no such thing."

Ulrick laughed. "You did not have to, my friend. Your appearance speaks for itself."

"What is wrong with the way I look?" Killian snarled before looking down upon his clothes to see what was out of place.

"Hair cut and combed, beard gone, and wearing your best tunic tells everyone here of your plans to court some fair lady," Ulrick winked with a wicked smile. "You should make haste. Go and claim the Lady Ella."

His innards clenched into knots when he saw her dance partner place his hand lower than Killian thought was respectful. "Can ye not see for yerself she is already spoken for?"

"I am not necessarily speaking about who she is dancing with at this very moment, my friend."

Killian looked upon the younger man next to him. "Aye, she is spoken on that account as well," he grumbled. His disposition soured further with this discussion.

"Is she?"

"Of course, she is, ye fool. I have spent time with the lady in the past but all who reside here at Berwyck knows the lady is but waiting for a certain point in time for her tae be reunited with the one she loves."

"Mayhap she knows not what she wants. She's been wandering the land for many a year. People change," Ulrick stated with a knowing look.

"Not when they are in love."

"And yet she has not been near nor seen this man for how long?" he asked. "Perchance her fate has altered and she does not even know this as yet. I think Lady Katherine would probably say this is something akin to star-crossed lovers or some such rot from one of her love stories."

"Leave it be, lad," Killian muttered into his drink.

Ulrick shrugged, standing to leave the table. "'Tis your

choice, but if you have any feelings for the lady, now would be the time to profess them before 'tis too late."

"I never said I had feelings for the woman."

"Again... you did not have to," Ulrick repeated with a slap upon Killian's back before he took his leave to join the dancing.

As Killian watched Ella being escorted back to the head table, he downed his drink. He had never been one to turn down a challenge, not that Ulrick dared him to do something repulsive. He stood and began making his way through the hall. After all, how horrible could it be to ask the woman for just one dance?

CHAPTER 3

Ella's nerves were on edge. That must be why she was feeling so anxious when she noticed Killian making his way across the hall. She reached for her chalice of wine, her fingers trembling before she managed to wrap them around the cup to take a sip without the heady red liquid spilling all over her gown. Perchance she should excuse herself and seek her chamber to rest. That was all she needed. She just had to go and rest before she left Berwyck forevermore to finally meet her destiny.

"He favors you," Amiria's voice was a soft whisper barely heard above the lutes playing in her hall.

There was no point in denying that she knew whom Amiria meant. "You are mistaken," Ella replied taking another sip from her goblet before setting it upon the table. She clutched her hands together upon her lap, her knuckles quickly becoming white. Her heart tapped a ferocious beat inside her chest. This was *not* happening! Not when she was this close to being reunited with the one man she had crossed time for.

Amiria reached over to clasp her hands, giving them a slight squeeze. Ella turned to look upon her friend, who had given her shelter more times than she could count over the years. Amiria was a beautiful woman with flaming red hair and eyes of violet. She reminded Ella of a Viking shield maiden of old, since Amiria could wield a sword as no other woman of Ella's acquaintance.

"I have waited many a year for some woman to catch his eye," Amiria replied, her tone conveyed all the love she felt for the man who had watched over her like her father would have done if he yet lived.

Ella saw Killian's progress was interrupted when he began having speech with Gregory, another of Dristan's knights. "I have not caught his eye, my lady. Besides you know my fate lies in another direction."

Amiria sighed, leaning over towards her husband when he whispered in her ear. She began to rise but bent over to kiss Ella's cheek. "Be kind to him, Ella. I do not wish to see him hurt."

Before Ella could make any reply, Amiria left to dance with her husband. They were an impressive pair, the two of them, and she was happy the couple twirling across the floor had found true love. Everyone deserved to find the person who called to them, soul to soul, Ella included.

Killian stood in front of the table clearing his throat, bringing her back to the challenge before her. "Mayhap ye would favor me with a dance, Ella?"

He appeared nervous, but the smile she gave him was genuine when he willingly dropped the whole *lady* business and called her only by her first name. "Aye, of course, Killian."

His faced showed the briefest glimpse of relief before a mask of indifference fell into place. He came around the table, gave a courtly bow, and then offered his arm. Hesitant, but curious if she would have the same reaction as when she had touched him earlier, she placed her hand in the crook of his elbow. Her breath hitched at their contact. How could this be happening? She did not understand what was going on with the man who began ushering her through the patterns of a lively tune.

The other dancers upon the floor became a blur, her partner the only one who remained in focus. Each time they came together and touched, small sparks flowed like the sweetest nectar through her body. The sensation warmed her entire being, making it hard to remember the steps of the dance. Her wits surely must be addled as she continued to gaze into the hypnotizing eyes of her partner.

Killian was an accomplished dancer, of that there could be no doubt, despite him always showing the outside world a gruff appearance. He took her by the waist and lifted her high while the dance continued, his arms of steel more than capable of easily picking her up as though she weighed nothing at all. As he lowered her back to the floor, her eyes widened as she slid down his body. Her hands remained on his shoulders as they just stood there, the dance all but forgotten.

"Ella, I—"

The door of the keep slammed open, causing all eyes to turn in the direction to see who would enter Lord Dristan's domain with such a loud ruckus. It was him! He had found her! Her fingers clenched in Killian's tunic to keep herself from falling to the ground. Was the room suddenly stifling with heat? She wavered on unsteady legs, feeling faint for the first time in her life. Yet, Killian came to her rescue, sweeping his arm around her waist before she fell when her knees began to buckle.

"Let me help ye, Ella," his voice held nothing but concern as they made their way to a chair against the wall. Calling for wine, he thrust the chalice in her direction once the goblet was filled. The wine sloshed over the rim and he cursed his clumsiness when the red wine barely missed her gown. "My apologies," he muttered, worry etched upon his face.

Taking the goblet, she gulped at the wine. Between trying to catch her breath and attempting to swallow, she began to choke on the drink. Killian started patting her back as though this would help but 'twas a bit too forceful to be of much use. "Killian, please…" she gasped while holding out her hand for him to stop. Her eyes darted about the room once she could breathe again, and yet a sense of panic radiated from every fiber of her being. She was anything but calm.

"I must be an imbecile tae think I could offer ye some form of aid without doing ye harm," he said with furrowed brow.

"'Tis not a matter of you not helping me, but please, I beg of you, do not leave my side."

He muttered words beneath his breath before his eyes traveled to the knight who had made his way to the lord and lady of the keep. "Ye know of him?" he asked, and Ella could see for herself he was sincere in his worry for her well-being.

"Yes," she answered, only to realize she had carelessly used modern speech. Her eyes widened in fright. Her body began to tremble and Killian took one of her hands in his. He began rubbing his callused thumb across its back, calming her nerves only a bit but still offering soothing relief all the same.

"I shall keep ye safe, Ella." Killian pulled her closer while her whole body began to shake. He leaned down to whisper in her ear. "Who is he?"

Ella raised her eyes to the Scotsman sitting beside her, knowing in her heart he would keep her from harm. A heavy sigh escaped her when she realized her past life had finally caught up with her.

"He's my son."

CHAPTER 4

Faramond of Hull bowed low before the lord of Berwyck Castle. He had not traveled this far north to just pay a friendly visit to a man known for his skill upon the battlefield. Nay, not this day. He had no time for such pleasantries and he was beyond tired of traveling from castle to castle bowing low before other lords when he himself was their equal.

He was on a mission of grave import and that was to bring his errant mother home. 'Twas of no matter he thought of her as the witch he called her all those years ago. His opinion of her had not changed.

She was a witch. She had cast a spell on his father, so that he had placed Faramond in the hands of a man who... Faramond would not think of it.

His only reason for continuing his quest to find his dame was to marry her off according to the king's demands so that he could reclaim his lands and the fortune held by his king if he were to succeed!

For nigh unto ten summers, Faramond had been considered only a steward of his own damn castle while he searched for the woman who had given him life. How one woman evaded him for so long was beyond his ken, and if he did not find her soon, all would be forfeit. He refused to lose after all he had schemed and accomplished to keep his holdings in his name. Nothing would stand in his way, and this included his missing mother.

"My lord and lady, I am Faramond of Hull," he announced when he rose from his courtly bow. "I thank you for receiving me."

"All are welcome here at Berwyck. You are far from home, Sir Faramond. What brings you so close to Scotland's borders?" Dristan asked while sipping his wine.

His teeth clenched at the lack of title. 'Twas obvious the man before him was no fool and knew of him. "I do not wish to take you away from your evening festivities but I am here on a matter of urgency."

"And what, pray tell, is of such import?" The Dragon of Berwyck stood, shared a look with his lady, before moving around the raised dais to stand before Faramond. He was an opposing figure but Faramond would not show any sign of weakness.

"I pray you may know of the whereabouts of my mother, the Lady Ella of Hull. Is she perchance in residence here at Berwyck?" he asked, hoping his face showed concern instead of the contempt he felt for the witch.

"Nay, I know not of any woman who goes by the name of Lady Ella," Dristan replied. Steel grey eyes peered at him as though he could see Faramond's true reason for seeking his mother.

"I am most worried for her safety. She has gone missing for many a year."

"I am sorry I am unable to help you locate her, but you are welcome to join us. I am sure Cook can get you something to eat if you are hungry, or I can have a chamber readied for you for the night."

Faramond gazed about the hall. "Food and a place to rest would be most welcome, my lord, before I continue my quest come the morn."

"Then come. Let me find you a table so you may eat your fill while I send a servant to stoke the fire in a room for you."

Lord Dristan left him no alternative but to follow along, but Faramond would do his own searching come the morn before he traveled on to the next castle. He would find his mother or die trying.

CHAPTER 5

Killian moved to stand before Ella. She was uneasy when she witnessed her son having speech with Dristan. 'Twas apparent she had no wish to see him, and Killian was more than happy to block her from her son's view. Dristan took the man to the far end of the hall while Killian continued to keep a wary eye on him.

Amiria rose and gave him a nod towards the turret stairs, which she began to climb. As a servant passed near at hand, Killian halted her from her task. "Fira, be a good lass and let me borrow yer shawl."

"Ye shall return it?" she asked while fingering the faded fabric. "'Twas my mother's."

"Aye, ye have my word."

The young woman unfastened the knot that had kept the garment in place and handed it over to Killian. He quickly placed the soft wool over Ella's head. "Come with me," he ordered, keeping his arm around her shoulder and guiding her towards the turret stairs.

Once out of sight and on the third floor of the keep, Killian turned towards Ella, whose eyes widened when he pushed her up against the stone wall of the passageway. "Ye have a son? Why in God's name, woman, are ye wandering around the countryside all these years if ye have a son who would protect ye?"

"Stop shouting at me, Killian," she seethed.

"I am not shouting!"

"Aye, you are! I am not someone to be man handled or bullied into submitting to your questions like one of the knights you train upon the lists." She pushed at the arm he had holding her in place 'til he at last released her.

He remained standing close to her side, giving her no alternative but to listen to him. Considering just moments before she had fear scattered across her lovely face, he saw no evidence of such weakness now. Her lips were pursed together as though she was battling whether or not she should continue to berate him. Killian had a hard time trying not to laugh while she attempted to contain her anger. She never appeared more beautiful.

"Ye try my patience, woman. All these many years of knowing ye and I had no idea ye had a son," he grumbled, taking his hand and wiping it across his brow.

"No one knows. He is all but dead to me. As far as I am concerned, I have no son."

"Well, he certainly is claiming ye as his mother despite ye wanting nothing tae do with him. Whatever he wants, he is more than willing tae go the whole length of England tae find ye, especially him being this far north."

"I care not what he wants from me." She gave him another push to put more distance between them but Killian barely moved.

Killian continued to watch her closely. Unshed tears pooled in her eyes. "What are ye not telling me? What did yer son do that was so horrible he continues tae have a hold over yer heart even though ye do not claim him as kin?"

"I do not wish to speak of it. Leave it be, Killian." Ella gave a low moan of anguish, her inner turmoil clearing rushing across her features once more.

"I think ye need tae unburden yer soul for I can see for myself ye have been holding yer emotions in check long enough," Killian murmured. "Tell me what he did."

A snarl burst from her lips like a wounded animal before she pounded her fists upon his chest. "Faramond threw me out of my own castle. That is what he did!"

"Why would he dishonor ye, his own mother, in such a manner?" he urged her to continue.

"I had confessed my true origins after my husband passed. My own son called me a witch and sent me from the only place I felt safe. I had nothing but the clothes on my back, the damn bloody bastard," she cried out, collapsing in his arms in a heap of despair.

Her tears tore at his heart, for he had not heard such suffering in many a year. Aye, she had indeed held her emotions in for far too long, if the river of tears soaking his tunic was an example of how she was feeling. He picked her up, even though she protested while still clutching at his tunic. She weighed next to nothing as he carried her to one of the window seats set into the rock wall. Keeping her on his lap, he leaned over to open the shutter to let in the ocean breeze.

She hiccupped, still trying to take in huge gulps of air to calm herself. She made an attempt to disengage herself from his arms but he only tightened them around her. "Dinnae fash yerself, Ella. I vowed I would keep ye safe and keep ye safe I shall, even it if means I must needs take ye myself tae see yer lover."

Where such a commitment came from, Killian had no idea. Now that he had made the promise, he was not sure if he would be able to just stand idly by while he handed the woman he cared about over to another man. He had never acknowledged his feelings towards Ella to anyone but himself, but she had unknowingly owned his heart for several years now. How could he have confessed such inner yearnings when he knew she pined away for another?

"He was never my lover," she murmured, almost giving him hope. Wiping her eyes, she gazed upon him sheepishly before scooting off his lap. "I am most sorry for breaking down in such a manner. I do not know what came over me, for I always thought I was made of sterner stuff. What you must think of me." She turned her head to look out at the dark night sky.

"Ella…"

"This is so embarrassing." She buried her face in her hands to hide from him.

"Ella…" He tried again to coax her to look upon him. When his words failed, he reached over, took her hands from her face, and tipped her chin up so he could see directly into her eyes.

His only thought was to give her the reassurance she needed, that he would keep her safe. But as he searched her face while staring into her trusting eyes, he knew he was forever lost. He was about to tell her they would ride out before the dawn. Truly, such was his intention. But as he watched her lips part to draw a deep breath, any thoughts of remaining level headed fled in that one instant as the time and space between them seemingly stood still.

He knew he would regret his rash decision, but Killian did not care. To hell with what he should and should not do! He would take and treasure this one moment, for he knew her heart belonged to another. But right now, in this very instant, Ella belonged to him. Without any further thought, and before he changed his mind, he lowered his head to kiss her lips.

CHAPTER 6

Ella had known the moment Killian had picked her up that something had shifted inside her world. Surely such a sensation was caused by her despair at seeing her son for the first time in many years. She could not deny Faramond's presence had rattled her wits. What kind of a mother was she that she was afraid of her own flesh and blood? How had she failed him?

But thoughts of her son drained away the instant Killian pressed his lips against her own.

Their breaths mingled on a heartbeat. Soft. Gentle. Searching. 'Twas an exploration of two beings trying to find one another while a rush of excitement shivered within their souls. A groan escaped her parted lips as she drew in her next breath. Never before had she felt such a deep yearning as she did now.

She knew what it was to live on the outside, yearning for the romance that had passed her by. This kiss was outside of her experience.

Killian must have taken the sound as encouragement for his arms wrapped around her bringing her closer. She reached out to cup his cheek, feeling the stubble of growth across her fingertips, while her other arm snaked around his neck. Her fingers curled into his hair as though she were holding onto him for support. She could feel his hand as it made its way through her hair with a caress. Slanting her head, he took full advantage of the opportunity presented to him as his tongue plunged into her mouth to dance with her own.

If Ella had not been sitting down, she surely would have fallen to the ground in a heap of pleasure. Wave after wave of desire coursed through her as though she had craved this man's touch her entire life. He made her forget everything but this moment. She cared not when he lifted her once again and she found herself sitting upon his lap. His arms wrapped themselves around her once more and she felt as if she were secured in a cocoon of warmth and comfort. He made her feel safe for the first time in more years than she could remember and she gave herself completely to this man who had addled her wits with just one kiss.

She gulped in air when his lips traveled to her neck. How long had it been since someone had actually made her *feel*? She whispered his name and all the sensations coursing through her body came to a screeching halt. He pushed her from his lap and Ella opened her eyes to stare at him in confusion. Her eyes widened when she realized her mistake.

Killian quickly stood and stepped back. The space between them was far greater than the few footsteps he had taken to distance himself from her. "I am *not* Henry," he muttered through clenched teeth.

His words, although uttered quietly, sounded to her ears as

though he bellowed them from the parapet high above the castle keep. "Aye, I know. I am sorry," she murmured, not sure how she could mend the hurt flashing across his angry face. She had wounded him deeply and such had not been her intention.

"'Tis my own fault. I knew yer heart belonged tae another. I will not again make the mistake of thinking ye could come tae care for me."

"'Tis not about how I feel for you, Killian. You have been a friend to me since I first walked inside Berwyck's gates."

"Ack... a friend." He gave a sarcastic chuckle. "I have always been just a friend tae ye and that is the way I should have kept what we have between us. I promise ye I shall not attempt tae kiss ye again."

"Killian, please... Let me explain," Ella attempted to placate him, but 'twas of no use. Whatever had briefly passed between them was now completely gone and 'twas all her fault.

"Nay. There is nothing tae explain, Ella. 'Tis obvious yer heart belongs tae another and I will see tae it ye are returned tae his side. Now, come. Amiria awaits us in her solar." He held out his hand motioning towards the passageway.

"I cannot see Amiria now." She touched her sensitive lips for she swore she could still feel Killian's mouth upon her own. She knew without a doubt Amiria would take one look at her and know something had happened between Ella and Killian. Shame coursed through her, knowing she had momentarily been unfaithful to the man she fell through time to be with.

"Then I will see ye tae yer chamber and explain tae Amiria we will leave before dawn breaks. An early departure should give us a fair enough lead before yer son attempts tae follow or find us."

True to his word, he escorted her down the corridor 'til they stood before her door, the silence between them crackled like lightning bolting across a thunderous sky. He put his hand upon the latch to open the portal for her but she unthinkingly put her own hand upon his arm to halt his progress. Before she thought better of her actions, she wound her arms around his waist and rested her head upon his chest.

"Thank you for escorting me tomorrow, Killian," she whispered. "I have been wanting to be reunited with him for a long time."

He mumbled something beneath his breath she could not make it out, and yet he at last took hold of her in a fierce embrace. Such comfort did not last long. He took her by her arms to pull her away only an instant later. Yet, he did not let go but instead rested his forehead against her own before heaving a weary sigh.

"Ye may be thanking me for taking ye tae him, but, honestly, I do not think ye really know what ye truly want, Ella," he declared. His tone was so sincere and Ella realized she had hurt him once more.

Before she could make any attempt to answer, he placed a quick kiss upon her forehead, reached behind her to open the door and gave her a gentle push inside her chamber.

"Bolt the door and get some rest," he ordered, his face bland to mask his feelings. But she could see them laid bare before her with just one look. Aye, he was hurt and she was to blame. "The morn will be upon us before ye know it."

The door shut and with its closing Ella felt as though all energy went rushing from her body. She put the bolt in place, her hand lingering on the wood. Only then did she hear Killian's footsteps receding down the passageway.

Her heart still racing, she all but put fell into a chair set by the hearth. Tears of regret pooled in her eyes before they fell down upon her cheeks. Why did she, of a sudden, feel so despondent Killian was gone from her side? She was getting what she wanted, was she not? The only thing that had kept her sanity all these years was the thought of being with Henry once more.

For nigh unto thirty years her only thoughts had been to stay alive so she would one day be able to return to his side to become his wife. She had even married another man for the sake of her great love, binding herself to the twelfth century.

She smiled at the memory of their first encounter at a quiet countryside tavern. He had entered the dimly lit room and he had told her later he had been blinded to anyone but her upon first espying her sitting at a corner table. Terrified and alone, she nodded to the vacant seat when he offered to buy her meal if she would but spare this mortal a few moments of her time.

Simon had charm and an abundance of it to flatter any woman who crossed his path. But he had been smitten with her from the start and wasted no time in pressing his suit in his favor. He had known from the very beginning she loved another. In fact, she made it clear her heart was spoken for. Yet he still professed his love would not falter and swore to protect her all of her days if she would but agree to marry him.

They wasted little time in seeking out a priest to bless their union and even less time before she was pregnant with their son. Simon had been faithful to her, as far as she knew, 'til the day of his passing. If only she could have come to love him as much as he professed to love her.

She had lived all these years for the chance to change the ending of her encounter with Henry. If she had stayed to persuade him instead of running, she would never have fallen into a time slip, and lost this past thirty years. It had been the mistake that shaped the rest of her life. Why, then, did she feel as though ignoring her attraction to Killian was the biggest mistake of her entire existence?

CHAPTER 7

The hours before dawn left a chill in the air. Two saddled horses whinnied as though in protest they were no longer in the warmth of the stable. Killian made his way to them, checking the leather straps to ensure everything was secure. Once he was satisfied the lads had done a proper job, he saw that his belongings and some foodstuff were tied to the back of the saddle.

His black horse stomped its front hoof before pawing at the ground. Nostrils flaring, he snorted, turning his breath to a light mist from the frigid morn. He nudged Killian, who brought his hands to his mouth to blow his own warm air into them to take the chill from his fingers. He gave the steed a pat.

"'Twill do ye no good tae be complaining, Mystic. Ye may not care ye are out at this hour but we are traveling this day whether ye like it or not." Killian received another push, causing him to voice his displeasure at the animal. "Behave, ye ornery beast," he scolded. Mystic nickered and shook his glorious black mane as though laughing at his master.

Killian had just secured his weapons on his horse when he saw Ella, Amiria, and Dristan approaching.

"You must make haste, Killian," Dristan said, carrying a torch to light their way. "I cannot vouch for how long we can keep Faramond occupied before he decides to continue his search for Lady Ella."

Amiria and Ella hugged one another. "Killian will keep you safe," Amiria declared, "but you must ride hard and fast to put as many miles between you and your son."

Killian watched Ella's face blanch in the torch light. "Ride? I cannot ride," she huffed. "Why do you think I have walked wherever my feet would take me?"

"Ye never learned tae ride?" Killian asked, trying not to curse.

"There was never any need. Besides, I am perfectly capable of walking or riding in a cart."

"*God's Bones*, woman! We have no time tae be walking nor taking a leisurely ride about the countryside in a wagon," Killian growled. "Or would ye rather have yer son take ye back tae Hull?"

"You are shouting at me again," Ella answered, crossing her arms on her chest.

"I am not!"

"Aye, you are, and now you find it necessary to argue with me as well."

Killian clenched his fists trying to calm down. She was so frustrating at times. "Then answer me," he said calmly, although he was anything but calm. "Do ye wish tae be taken tae Hull?"

"You already know the answer to your question. Besides…

you promised to keep me safe and take me to Henry. Are you going back on your vow?"

"Ye know I am doing no such thing."

Ella smiled as though the argument had been won in her favor. "Then we shall be walking."

She began to stroll past Killian but he grabbed her arm. "Nay, we ride," he ordered.

Dristan stepped forward. "If the two of you would cease your squabbling, you would both realize neither of you will win your point. Ella, you cannot walk all the way to your destination in time for the appointed hour when everything you have waited for and said will occur. Further, you will be caught. I do not know what Faramond is up to, but I know he is not to be trusted. Killian, you know very well this situation is not a time for a lesson on how to ride a horse."

Amiria ordered a stable lad to fetch a pillion before giving Ella a nudge towards Killian. "Enough of this. You know I love you both but you are driving me mad. I have never met two such stubborn people more made for each other than the two of you."

Dristan laughed. "I might argue such a point, my love." He took the cushion from the lad when he returned and attached it behind Killian's saddle.

Amiria joined in his merriment and poked him in the chest. "You and I will settle this later in the lists, my lord. As for you two," she said pointing towards the horses, "Ella will ride with Killian. You can tether the other horse and switch off as they tire."

"But my lady—" Ella began to protest but Killian lifted her up onto the pillion.

"He will keep his promise, Ella. Trust him and trust what is in your heart," Amiria said.

Dristan clasped Killian's hand. "Make for Warkworth. Riordan and Katherine will give you shelter so the horses can rest before you must travel again."

Killian nodded before Amiria came to embrace him in a fierce hug. She tugged on his tunic and he leaned down so she could whisper in his ear. "All will work out as it should, Killian. Do not lose hope that you can still have your heart's desire."

"How did you know?" he murmured in puzzlement. How could this woman he had known since she was a mere bairn read him so openly?

"We women just know these things." She kissed his cheek before returning to her husband's side. "God speed and return to us soon."

Killian tied Ella's horse to his saddle before he mounted. Ensuring the woman was as comfortable as possible, he waved his hand in farewell. A slight motion of his heel and they were on their way as his horse obeyed his command to move. With the closing of the barbican gate, Killian picked up the pace and made for the beach. Dawn would break soon and he would make use of the blanket of darkness to keep them concealed. They would need to ride hard. Daylight would soon be upon them.

CHAPTER 8

Faramond awoke, irritated his slumber was disturbed by some unknown force. His nose twitched and he waved his hand in front of his face to get rid of whatever had been annoying him in his sleep. Instead of perchance encountering an insect buzzing around his head, his fingers came in contact with long strands of brown hair before he remembered how he had spent what he could recall of the night. The wenches at Berwyck were certainly most accommodating, or at least one was.

Ale had flowed freely last eve, especially after Lord Dristan ordered a keg brought up from the cellars. His knights had appeared more than happy the festivities continued far into the early morn. Faramond had hoped the drink would loosen their tongues so he could glean some information his mother had visited Berwyck at some point. Unfortunately, all his questions only earned him another round as his tankard was refilled again and again. 'Twas not long before his head began to spin and he made his way up to his chamber.

He had been more than a little surprised to see the woman who now lay next to him hovering near his chamber door last eve. She was a good-looking woman, although he had bedded prettier. She had held a pile of linens as if she were about some chore, but in his mind's eye 'twas but an excuse for what she really wanted. With her come hither gaze and her eyes all but stripping the clothes off his body, he had opened the door to let her choose if she entered or not. If she was offering to service him, Faramond was not fool enough to deny himself a bit of sport!

She began to stir, curling her arms around him as though taking possession of him, not that she could. Faramond had no desire to be tied down to any woman who would not bring with her a great deal of wealth to line his coffers. But a slight deviation from his plan to rise early to continue his search could be delayed, especially when the woman moved atop of him. *Aye, she is most accommodating*, Faramond thought again, as he guided her about their play to show her what he liked. She did not seem to mind that he enjoyed his pleasure a little rough while she made every effort to please him.

She began nibbling upon his neck and uttering useless words of love. Not wishing to hear such endearments from a woman who was no more than a whore, he grabbed her and lifted her beneath him as he plowed into her softness over and over again. A sudden gasp escaped her when Faramond spilled his seed, not caring the woman had not found her own release.

He pulled off her and rose from the bed, ignoring the look of disappointment flashing briefly across her features. He began to don his clothing even while she reached for the fur coverings to hide her nakedness.

"Ye be leavin' so soon?" Her slight Scottish brogue was a

grim reminder of how close he was to Scotland's border. He would much rather be sitting in front of his own damn hearth breaking his fast.

"I must ride. I am searching for my mother," he answered, trying to remember if they had even had this conversation before. Nay, they wasted little time on speech last eve before they fell into bed. "Perchance you know of her. She is called Lady Ella of Hull."

The brassy wench had the nerve to look upon him as though she were bored. "Do ye even remember my name?" she asked, all but ignoring his question. Her brow rose awaiting his answer.

He swiped the back of his neck attempting to recollect what she was called, not that it mattered. He would forget her as soon as he left Berwyck's gates far behind. "Fire," he replied when the name finally came to him.

"Fira," she huffed.

"Close enough." He came closer to the bed. "Do you know of her?"

Fira fluffed the pillows behind her, settled back into the bed, and then pulled one corner of the coverlet down. She patted the vacant space next to her in an invitation to join her. "Sit," she urged, "or better yet, come back tae bed. Surely there are much better ways tae be spending yer morn than traipsing about the countryside."

Faramond watched in amusement when she let the coverlet fall below her naked breasts. Reaching out, he gave one pink puckered nipple a pinch, enjoying the sound of her startled surprise. A wicked gleam entered her eyes and she licked her lips.

"You have not answered me," Faramond muttered, taking

hold of her other breast and giving the bounty he held in his hand a rough squeeze. He had the distinct impression this woman knew exactly whom he was speaking about.

Fira shrugged and then proceeded to examine her nails. "Everyone at Berwyck knows Ella, although she insists she is no lady and even refuses tae answer tae such a title. I heard tell she was leaving before dawn. Heading south, I think, tae be reunited with some man she loves, or so goes the whisperings I overheard with the kitchen servants."

A snarl burst from Faramond's lips. "*Bloody hell*! You have all conspired against me!" He began rushing around the chamber collecting his gear.

"Ye cannae leave without me," Fira yelled out.

"Aye, I can." He went to the shutter shoving it open. Cursing, he realized he had slept the morn away and 'twas far later than he thought.

She pushed the covers off her and rushed to his side. "Ye promised me last eve if I gave myself tae ye, then ye would take me with ye."

A snort escaped him. "I did no such thing."

"Aye, ye did, milord. Ye said ye would make me the lady of yer castle." Rubbing her naked body against him did not have the effect she had apparently been hoping for. He had no intentions of changing his mind, even if he had uttered such nonsense.

He laughed. "You silly fool. What makes you think I would take a common whore for a wife?"

"But what if there is a bairn from our coupling?" She began wringing her hands together.

"What makes you think I would believe the brat was mine?"

Her chin quivered, tears welling in her eyes. "But ye promised…"

"You should have learned years ago to live with disappointment. Promises are always made to be broken." Enough people had broken promises to him. His father and mother, for a start. The knight to whom he'd been sent for fostering. The king. Every stupid wench that swore she loved him with one eye on his purse.

He picked up his sword and strapped the blade to his side. Reaching into the leather pouch, he fetched a coin and tossed the money onto the bed. "Payment for your services. It should be enough to keep you off your back for a while."

He left her without a backwards glance. The only sound of her annoyance was the shattering of something she threw upon the closed portal.

He had wasted enough time this morn. Making his way through the great hall, he grabbed a loaf of bread off a nearby table and headed out the door to the inner bailey. He summoned a lad to fetch his horse. He would head south in the hopes this was the direction his mother was going and that Fira spoke no falsehood. After all… how far could a woman wander on foot?

CHAPTER 9

Dusk had fallen, the sky a heavenly splash of color in rich pink and purple. Every part of Ella's body gave a silent scream of protest. She had had enough of the beast beneath her. Her fingers clenched Killian's tunic to the point her knuckles were white while she continued to hold on as if her life depended on it. Who was she kidding? She was afraid to let go for she was certain she would find herself slipping from the horse and possibly breaking a bone or two during her descent to the ground. This riding a horse business was better left to those who grew up around the wretched animals from the time they could first walk.

During the hours of their travel, Killian had kept, for the most part, silent. The only exception was a word or two encouraging her that her time in the saddle would soon be at an end. They were making good progress on their journey south. But no matter how many times he said they would reach their destination shortly, Warkworth Castle was nowhere in sight. 'Twas obvious they would not reach its gates this eve and she could blame no one but herself since she had insisted on resting on several occasions.

Every step of Killian's steed, whether 'twas the fast or slow pace of the animal, brought its own obstacles, at least in Ella's mind. 'Twas difficult to remain a respectable distance from a man when you were sitting upon his lap. She had given up sitting on the pillion behind him hours ago, and Killian's saddle left no other alternative than to be wrapped within his embrace while he steered his horse in the direction of their destination. At one point she had insisted she ride upon the rump of the horse to at least put an end to the intimacy of their close proximity. Yet Killian would not hear of it. 'Twas either she settle herself in her current location or she rode her own horse. The ride all the way to Conisbrough Castle seemed as though 'twould be a long endless journey.

"Enough, Killian. Please... I beg of you. I cannot sit another minute on this beast from hell," Ella complained in a soft whisper.

He pulled on the reins bringing the horse to a halt and scanned the perimeter of the area. "We shall make for the trees tae conceal us. Can ye ride just a few more minutes, Lady Ella?" he asked.

She rested her head upon his chest and felt his arms tighten around her. "Once I am upon solid ground again, I will give you a sound verbal thrashing for using the *L* word with me again. 'Til then, I suppose my bruised backside can withstand a few more minutes of torture on this hideous creature."

Mystic whinnied, causing Killian to chuckle while he turned his mount towards the nearby trees. "You treat me as if I am but a naughty child and then insult my horse. Whatever am I tae do with you, Ella?"

That question could have so many different meanings, she thought, even while she listened to the beat of his heart beneath her ear. Even her own traitorous emotions were a mess while he held her. She should be thinking of being reunited with Henry instead of pondering the horrible task of saying goodbye to Killian. He had always been so very kind to her and she would miss his company when she no longer journeyed to Berwyck.

"Ella?"

Her name as it passed his lips was like a promise to her ears. A promise he would keep her safe. A promise he would keep his vow. A promise of something more, if she would but forget everything she had fought so hard to hold on to all these years. It had been so long since she had seen the man she crossed time for. Could she even remember every detail of his face? His memory had, for the most part, become just a blur in her mind, and yet her heart still cried out for him. Why? 'Twould be so easy to forget aught else but Killian. And yet, Henry had been the reason she was in twelfth-century England in the first place, and the only reason she remained.

For years she had kept to her purpose of remaining in the past. Her greatest fear had been that dwelling on thoughts of her life in the future might tear her back to the twenty-first century, instead of being reunited with her long-lost love.

Aye... love him she had, but how could she have known that her doubts they could have a life together would tear them apart? Their time together had been riddled with conflict, even though they had spent two months falling in love with one another. First, she had to accept she had really fallen through time, and Henry needed to stop believing she was not a witch. But there was a bigger problem.

The king was demanding that Henry marry a younger woman of considerable wealth. When the woman had showed up at Henry's castle, Ella had run, tears streaming down her cheeks, into the nearest forest. Not looking where she was going, she plummeted once more through time, finding herself in the same century but thirty years earlier. And thirty years younger.

She lifted her head to gaze upon this man who had been such a dear friend to her all these years. His eyes filled with concern and she offered him a smile to set any fears he may have to rest. She would not burden him with the troubling thoughts going through her head. If she acted on her feelings for him, surely she would only live to regret such a rash decision. Her destiny was with another and not with this caring man before her.

"I will be fine, Killian. Let us just rest for the eve. Everything will look brighter in the morn."

He gave a nod and continued to steer his horse towards the trees. Relief flooded through Ella. She had the distinct feeling she would not be able to handle a deep conversation with Killian right now. Each time he gazed upon her, her heart leapt almost as though they could see into each other's souls. Such a revelation was not comforting when Ella continued to try to remind herself her heart belonged to another. Or did it? She rubbed at her eyes feeling the beginnings of a migraine.

They rode deeper into the forest longer than Ella would hope but finally Killian pulled on the reins, halting the animal beneath them. Night had now fallen, but Ella was used to the dark, for she had concealed herself for many a year by using little to no light. She had not survived as long as she had by not adjusting to her surroundings and her need to remain hidden, not only from her son, but from those who roamed the countryside and would physically harm her if they came upon her.

Killian dismounted and as Ella slid onto the hard saddle, she gave a low moan. He held out his arms to help her down yet even the slightest movement caused her pain. She placed her hands upon his shoulders, and his own went about her waist as he lifted her. She skimmed down his body and her own came alive at the sensation. Her breath caught in her throat. Her knees buckled when her feet met the ground, yet Killian only brought her firmly up against his chest to prevent her fall. She gasped even while her arms wrapped themselves around his neck to hold on for support. Before she could even comprehend what her traitorous heart was feeling, he quickly lifted her up.

"Killian! Put me down this instant," she ordered.

"And have ye fall when yer legs give out again? I think not."

"This is highly inappropriate," she barely choked out her reply before he adjusted her within his arms in order to pull a blanket from the gear on her horse.

"Ach! We are grown adults, Ella. Do ye honestly think I will let a woman in my care come tae harm?" he grumbled, making his way a short distance to a nearby log. "Dristan would have my head and I currently like its placement." He tossed the blanket upon the ground before kneeling down to gently set her upon it.

They stared one to the other, neither putting any distance between them. Her fingers automatically curled into the length of his hair, the softness pulling to her senses.

"Yer safe, my lady. Ye can let go now."

His words were lost to her just as surely as she had lost all sense of reality. "What?" she murmured.

He chuckled and gave her a truly wicked grin as though he knew where her thoughts had led. "I canna tend tae a fire if ye continue tae hold onto me, Ella."

He might as well have thrown a bucket of frigid water upon her. *Good heavens! What is coming over me*, she mused. She quickly tore her arms from around his neck and folded her shaking fingers in her lap. "Sorry," she muttered in embarrassment.

Killian wrapped the blanket around her. "No need tae be apologizing, Ella. Rest yerself and I shall tend tae camp."

"I can help," she said, starting to rise.

He gave her a gentle nudge on her shoulder. "Nay. There is no need. Ye are in my care so for once let someone take care of ye for a change."

"I am used to fending for myself."

He stood but watched her intently. "And I admire ye for it, but for now let me see tae keeping ye safe. Ye have fended for yerself far longer than ye should have."

He walked away leaving her there in the dark with her thoughts running amuck inside her head. Soon, a small fire was lit at her feet to take the chill of the night air away, but 'twas the sound of Killian's low singing of some Scottish song that lulled her into a peaceful sleep. She would have been startled to know that he observed her far into the night before he found his own slumber.

CHAPTER 10

His name, whispered in his ear like a soft caress, had Killian clasping the welcoming curves of the woman whose arms were draped around his shoulders. Kisses trailed down his neck, causing parts of him to stir to life and he inhaled the fragrance of her hair smelling of sweet flowers.

"Killian…"

The seductive tone of Ella's voice had Killian's mind imagining a life together. His dream seemed so real, especially considering how well she fit within his embrace. The intrusion of birds calling to one another high above the treetops in the early morning hours only caused Killian to grasp this woman closer to him for surely he did not wish to rouse from his slumber. Let him dream just a bit longer…

"Killian, my love…"

My love? His eyes burst open at such an avowal while Ella dreamed on. He was startled to find the lady was truly wrapped around him like a second skin. He had not been dreaming after all, for apparently they naturally claimed one another while they had slumbered.

He began to carefully disengage himself from Ella, but once again her words halted any thoughts of moving farther from her side.

"Kiss me, Killian," she murmured in her sleep.

He had made her a promise he would not kiss her again. He had every intention of honoring such a vow, and yet how could he deny himself the taste of her when she urged him closer with a gentle tug upon the back of his neck? He leaned forward to brush his lips against her own as if he had no choice but to honor her simple request. Yet there was nothing simple about what ignited between them. Fire erupted in his veins at the first encounter even while he heard a soft moan escaped her. 'Twas the sweetest sound he had ever heard but he also knew he would regret taking advantage of her in such a manner.

Their kiss ended sooner than he would have wished. Ella's eyes briefly flickered open, causing Killian to hesitate with an offer of an apology. Her smile brightened her whole countenance, but such a look was fleeting and Killian knew she was still under the delusion she was dreaming. She gave a heavenly sigh, and then took up the fur pelt to return to her slumber.

Killian jerked back and slumped against the fallen log. A hundred scenarios raced across his mind while he attempted to figure out how in the hell he was ever going to turn over the woman he loved to another man. She *must* care for him. Why else would she whisper his name while she slept? He could not even think further upon her words when she uttered *my love*, let alone how she asked for his kiss. Aye, she may have been dreaming, but surely there was some truth hidden deep within her that she mayhap cared for him too.

Reaching for the pouch on his belt, he opened the leather and pulled out his mother's ring. 'Twas the only thing he had left of the woman who gave him life. For one instant, he thought of bestowing this treasure to Ella, but he quickly dismissed the idea knowing her heart went to another. But what if she had changed her mind?

A heavy sigh escaped him when he returned the ring to the pouch and pulled the leather straps closed. He was going to lose his mind before he found any form of answer to his questions, at least while arguing with himself in his own head. He stoked the fire and went off into the woods to see if he could catch something to break their fast, all the time thinking about having speech with Ella regarding her possible feelings for him. He might as well attempt to stay occupied instead of letting his mind run wild with thoughts of Ella belonging only to him. 'Twas either that or resign himself to the task of letting her go.

Ella awoke to the smell of something roasting over the crackling fire. She stretched, gave a yawn, and smiled in delight when she remembered the dream she had been having of Henry. *Henry...* she thought his name with a frown forming on her brow as she continued to awaken fully. Nay, 'twas not Henry she had been dreaming of at all but her traveling companion!

Her eyes flew open and immediately sought the man from her dreams. Killian had been observing her with what appeared keen interest but she did not expect the scowl marring his handsome features.

Handsome? Where the devil did such a thought come from and why did she continue to have recurring feelings, of a sudden, for Killian? Their kiss from her dream had seemed so very real, along with the rush of emotions carousing through Ella like the excitement of seeing the first bloom of a spring rose.

"G–good morn, K–Killian," she stammered, placing her shaking hands upon the ground to rise to a sitting position. *Good Lord!* She could not even form a sentence without sounding like a bumbling idiot. What had come over her? She pulled the blanket around her shoulders in order to have something to do and mayhap calm her frayed nerves.

He grunted a hasty good morn and continued turning the rabbit on a spit over the fire. He seemed irritated and yet Ella had no idea why.

"Is aught amiss?" she asked, almost afraid to hear his answer.

He opened and closed his mouth several times before shaking his head. "Nay. 'Tis nothing tae concern ye."

His gruff manner was completely out of character, unless he was cross with her, so Ella knew without any doubt she was the root of his foul mood. She wracked her brain in an attempt to figure out what she might have done to displease him. Perchance 'twas the delay in arriving at Warkworth that concerned him, as her son could be fast behind them for all they knew. "I am sorry I am not an accomplished rider, Killian, if this is why you are upset with me. I promise to be better today since I am now fully rested."

Killian tested the meat and then began to divide up their meal. He repeated the process several times before standing and handing her a metal plate. He went back to his place across the fire. The distance between them felt like he was miles away.

"Killian." His name left her lips and the sound reminded her of how she had spoken to him in her dream… actually she had yearned for him while she had slumbered. If she were to be honest with herself, she began to wonder how far off those feelings truly were. His eyes widened before his attention went back to his meal.

"If we ride hard, we should reach Warkworth's gates by late morn."

She set her plate down only to realize she had not even as yet taken a bite of the food he had prepared for her. "What is wrong?" She stood up and went to sit next to him. He, on the other hand, cursed something in Gaelic and jumped up putting the fire between them once more.

"There is nothing wrong. Ye should eat yer fill while ye have the chance. I willnae be stopping again 'til we reach Warkworth," he fumed and began pacing back and forth in agitation.

"If this is what you look like when nothing is wrong, I should hate to see you when you are cross!" She stood again and placed herself in front of him with hands upon her hips. But she was unprepared when he grabbed her arms and gave her a shake.

"Ye best leave the matter rest, woman," he yelled.

"I am not certain I like the way you call me *woman*. Why are you so angry with me?" Ella shouted back.

"Do ye not ken what ye be putting me through?" he snarled, clearly agitated about something she had done.

"I have no clue what you are grumbling about. You must be the most frustrating man I have ever come across. Was your slumber disturbed by rocks digging into your arse that you awoke so cross this morn?"

Ella did not miss the quick smirk that flashed across Killian's mouth before he hid his emotions with a grim look of displeasure.

"'Tis not rocks in my arse that be the problem, Ella."

"Then what is it?" she asked. Her eyes widened when his began to all but smolder and she began to quickly wonder if her dreams had in truth been a reality.

"'Twould be best to let the matter rest, Ella," he all but growled out again like a wounded animal.

"How can I? I demand to know what I have done to incur your wrath, you ornery man!"

"Ella—"

She took a step closer. "Tell me, Killian," she said taking a hold of his arm, "so I can make amends."

"There is only one way to make this aright and 'twill only complicate the matter."

"Tell me," she urged again.

"I canna do anything but show ye, even if it means I must go against my vow tae ye," he declared, as he dipped his head downward.

"Killian—" His named came out as a breathy whisper before his lips descended upon her own when he broke his own promise to never kiss her again.

His arms whipped around her in a fierce grip. His kiss deepened and she could do naught else but pour every ounce of energy into their meeting. A moan escaped her while she forgot everything else but the man who claimed her.

Aye, claim her he did, for no act was ever clearer than Killian's possession of her. Nothing else mattered other than how he was making her feel and yearn for the one thing that had been missing her entire life... love... if she would but succumb to what this man would offer her and forget her quest to find Henry.

His mouth plundered her own and excitement rushed

through her entire body even while her knees began to buckle. But she did not fall. Nay... how could she stumble when Killian held her so securely up against his own muscular body? Her own trembling body reacted to his nearness as her fingers clenched his tunic. She never wished for this moment to end.

Before she knew what he was about, he scooped her up at her knees and laid her down about her discarded blanket. He broke off their kiss and their eyes met. His breath and hers mingled together like one soul reaching out to the other. She ran her fingers through his hair before he tore her hands away. He stood to peer down upon her, his chest heaving as though he, too, had been just as affected by what had just occurred between them. Cool air waved its way across her body when he left her to move before the fire. For an instant she wanted to call him back to her side so she would be warm again.

"Do ye even know yer own mind, Ella, and what ye desire?"

"I know what I want," she answered jutting out her chin, as though protesting what was warring inside her own head regarding this man before her.

He laughed but 'twas not a merry sound that echoed off into the forest. "Nay... ye do not, as our kiss will attest. Ye best decide what, or who, ye be wanting before we meet up with yer man, else ye may be getting more from me than ye bargained for."

He went to his horse, grabbed one of the satchels, and then started to storm away.

"Where are you going?" she shouted at his retreating, angry form. Briefly, she worried he would leave her to her own devices. She could tell he was *that* angry.

"Tae find a cold stream," he shouted, entering the forest.

The situation appeared so comical that Ella would have

laughed if she had known he was no longer within hearing distance. Good heavens... what Killian did to her peace of mind would surely send her falling right back into his arms. She just might need to find the cold stream for herself upon his return. She could use a good dousing!

CHAPTER 11

Killian pulled back on Mystic's reins. The horse whinnied and snorted as the beast was halted upon a hill overlooking a village in the valley below.

"Awake, Ella," he coaxed with a low murmur to the woman he held. When his attempt failed, he gave her a small shake but she only pressed herself further into his body as though to find further comfort. "We are almost tae Warkworth."

Ella at last began to awake from her slumber, her head rising from its placement upon his shoulder. Her eyelids fluttered opened and in her place between wakefulness and her dreams, she bestowed upon him a smile so brilliant he forgot all else but the woman he had come to love. Aye, love her he did, which only caused him to grimace with the knowledge she would never belong to him.

"I am sorry, Killian," she said, sitting upright with an attempt to distance herself from him. "I did not even realize I had fallen asleep. Where are we?"

"As I mentioned, we are almost tae Warkworth," he answered pointing to the castle in the distance.

"I never thought to see the place again," she whispered.

"How long has it been since yer path crossed this way?"

"It has been some time. I've been wandering inland and staying away from any river ports in hopes I could avoid my son."

Killian clucked his tongue and pressed his knees into his steed, putting Mystic back into motion. They began to make their way down the hill and across lush green fields. "Have ye not missed Lady Katherine's company?"

"Aye, I have. She is like the daughter I never had and I miss her company greatly," Ella declared holding onto the pommel of the saddle as though such an act would keep her from bumping into Killian with each step the horse took. "She and Lord Riorden do not make their way to Berwyck as often as I would like, although I do understand his reluctance to allow her to venture too far from their home." She gave him a glance from the corner of her eyes.

"Ye mean given her origins?" he teased with a wink of conspiracy.

"You know from whence she hails?"

"Ye forget I have seen several of these future women come tae Berwyck's gates, yerself included, of course."

"Aye, of course you have. One must needs be careful where you put your feet else you may end up where you do not belong," she stated.

"'Tis obvious ye know a thing or two about such an occurrence."

"You know my story. You know I have been through Time not once but twice in my lifetime. I do not think I could stand another trip and am perfectly content to live out my remaining days firmly planted in the twelfth century," she answered with a slight shiver. "Sometimes I feel as though this century has been home to me far longer than my previous life far off into the future where I never fit in anyway."

"I wouldnae wish tae lose ye tae Time, Ella, so be careful where ye step," Killian declared pulling her closer.

"You would not?" she asked.

"Nay, madam, I wouldnae. If ye were gone from this world, who else would put up with my lively banter or handle my anger as well as ye do?" Killian's gruff reply had him biting back any further words that might tumble from his mouth. Surely he was sounding like a bumbling imbecile by even confessing even this small measure of desire on how he wished her to stay here in this time… with him.

"If only I had found you first…" she murmured then gave a gasp that she, too, had made such an admission.

Killian gave a sound deep in his chest as joy filled him that she had at last admitted there was something between them. He held his breath waiting for her to request him to turn his horse around and head back to Berwyck where they could live out their lives together. But there was nothing coming from her and he suddenly felt defeated in earning this woman's love.

"And yet ye still wish me tae deliver ye tae a man ye can barely remember." He groaned in dismay when his inner thoughts came tumbling unbidden from his mouth.

"Killian… please forgive me. I should have never revealed anything so personal nor spoken my feelings aloud."

"But voice them ye did, Ella. Are ye truly certain ye wish tae go on with yer plans? Is this really what ye wish in the deepest recesses of yer heart?"

Her eyes widened as though he had said something so vile she was offended at his words. "But I have been waiting for years to be rejoined with Henry again!" Her voice cracked and Killian was unsure if 'twas in outrage or because she was in truth reconsidering such a decision to press on with their journey.

"Plans change, as do hearts," he replied in a gruff tone.

"I have never considered myself so fickle that my heart could dismiss loving a man all my life and then easily go so thoughtlessly to another."

"And yet ye married a man in order tae stay in this time or did ye not consider *that* as a betrayal of this love ye bore a man ye barely knew for two months?" There was no mistaking the sarcastic tone to his voice.

Ella winced. "'Twas out of necessity, I assure you. I cared for Simon of Hull, and was a good wife to him."

"If ye say so," he grumbled, irritated she would not admit she cared for him and forget her notion to continue her journey onward.

"Who are you to judge me and the decisions I needed to make to ensure I stayed in this century?" she yelled out.

"I am the man that loves ye! That is who I am, ye stubborn woman," he bellowed.

Yanking on the leather reins, Killian's arms snaked around Ella when she lurched forward in the saddle at the abruptness of the horse coming to a sudden halt. Before he could think about how much he would once again regret his actions, Killian took hold of her face and crushed his lips onto her own.

'Twas meant to be a sort of punishment for her foolishness, and his own for loving a woman whose heart went to another. Yet the moment his mouth touched hers everything changed. No longer was he demanding a response from her in the way their tongues had initially warred with each other. Nay, he wanted her to give herself to him freely and of her own accord, so he would know for a certainty she wanted him as much as he wanted her.

He shifted Ella in his arms 'til their lips barely brushed against each other. Their breaths mingled together. Soft... searching... as he poured every bit of emotion he held for Ella into their kiss. He knew not how long they continued to plunder each other's senses but 'twas the low sultry moan of pleasure rumbling deep in her throat that caused Killian's heart to soar. She *did* care for him and he rejoiced knowing she had feelings for him.

Their breaths ragged, they opened their eyes simultaneously to stare in wonder by what they saw reflected. He cupped her cheeks, rubbing his callused thumbs across her smooth skin as though to memorize the planes of her features.

Killian pressed his forehead to hers while her arms wrapped themselves around his neck. "Admit it, lass..." he crooned softly, "ye care for me too."

She gave a heavy sigh before lifting her head. She ran her fingers down his cheek. The smile she bestowed upon him began at the edges of her lips before reaching her eyes. 'Twas such a look, as she searched his face, that gave him hope they might have a future together after all.

"Aye, Killian, I do care for you," she murmured, before resting her head once more upon his shoulder.

With a flick of the reins, Killian again set his horse into motion and 'twas not long before they were making their way through the village and up to Warkworth's barbican gate. As Mystic began clip clopping his way over the wooden bridge,

Killian observed Riorden and Katherine as they stood with a guest who appeared as though he was getting ready to depart from their company.

"Looks like they just had a guest," he said as he saw the knight double-checking his saddle cinches.

"I hope they do not mind we are barging in on them after they already had someone visiting," Ella answered. Raising her head she looked ahead into the bailey. "Oh my God!" she swore while sitting straight up in the saddle.

"What is wrong, Ella," Killian asked while he watched the scene before him with a sinking heart.

Riorden and Katherine's guest leapt into the saddle and bid them farewell but 'twas the woman swaying in his arms that confirmed his worst fears about exactly who the knight was. As he came abreast of them on the bridge, he halted his horse.

"Eh gads, man. Get your woman inside and let the Lady Katherine see to her. From the looks of her, you have been traveling far too long," he said, before clucking his tongue and kicking his horse back into motion.

Ella gasped for air. "Henry." His name, most likely torn from the depths of her soul, was barely heard, but, as far as Killian was concerned, she may just as well have shouted it for all of Christendom to hear.

He had no time to consider the implications of their chance meeting with the man Ella had said she crossed time for. He called out for the Lady Katherine when the lady he held fainted in his arms.

Faramond kicked at the ashes beneath his feet. Someone had

taken great care to dowse a fair amount of water on what had been left of the campfire. It could have been anyone, he supposed, and yet something in his gut told him his mother was not far from this very site.

He returned to his horse and continued onward on his journey with nothing but the sound of his own voice inside his head for company. Where was she and how many times over the years had he asked the same question? But he swore he would find her and soon. There were not many places left the woman could hide. If need be, he would return to Hull to get a fresh horse before continuing his quest to secure his future.

CHAPTER 12

Ella awoke with the softness of a feather bed beneath her. Her hand stroked the softness of the covering keeping her warm. Opening her eyes, she saw she was in the dimly-lit chamber she was used to occupying whenever her path crossed Warkworth's gates. As she had mentioned to Killian, she had not been here in some time.

A movement drew her attention to Lady Katherine sitting near the hearth. Her quill scratched its way across the parchment causing Ella to smile knowing the lady was surely working on one of the stories that constantly filled her head.

The coverlet began to move causing a startled gasp to pass her lips. Her fingers had not been pressed against a fur pelt but she had instead been caressing Killian's sleeping head. Their eyes met as he, too, awoke from his slumber. She swore her fingers burned where she had been touching him but 'twas nothing compared to the unmistakable heat radiating between them.

"Yer awake," he murmured coming to a stand.

"Aye."

"We was afraid ye might sleep the eve away," he continued. His voice sounded gruff, and once more annoyed with her.

"As you can see, such is not the case." Her skittish retort slipped through her lips before she could take them back, while his gaze continued to unnerve her.

Katherine came to her bedside. "I will see about getting you something to eat to break your fast. You must be starving for a hot meal now that you have rested from your travels."

Killian headed toward the door. "Nay, I will see tae it, Lady Katherine. I am certain ye would rather have speech together after Ella's long absence."

Katherine nodded and went to two chairs sitting next to the hearth. Sitting, she poured herself a chalice of wine and sipped while watching her and Killian with an amused smile. "Aye, we have lots to catch up on."

With Killian's departure, Ella got out of bed and made her way to sit in the vacant chair. Silence stretched between the two women while Ella determined how to begin their conversation. She had so much to ask and was not sure she really wished to know some of the answers. And then there was her confusion about the situation with Killian.

Katherine perused Ella with those skeptical aquamarine eyes. "He refused to leave your side when you passed out cold in his arms," she answered as if Ella had voiced her thoughts aloud.

"No glad greetings first, my friend," Ella muttered while running shaking hands across her face to hopefully clear her thoughts.

"Hi, Ella." Her tone was comical and so modern that Ella grimaced.

"Good day to you, my dear, or is it eve?"

"He refused to leave your side," she repeated with a raised brow, not answering her question as to the time of day... or night as the case may be. "Would you care to freely give me the details of what's going on with the two of you or do I need to force it out of you?"

"There is nothing going on with us. Killian is merely ensuring I reach my destination without coming to harm."

"*Right...*" Katherine said dragging out her word with a laugh. "If you say so."

"There is nothing to tell," Ella attempted again.

Katherine pulled her legs up onto her chair to get comfortable before pouring a chalice of wine and passing the cup to Ella. "If you wish to deny there is something going on between you and Killian, it's certainly none of my business, Ella."

"'Tis best you leave the matter alone, Katherine." As Ella said these words, she could hear Killian's voice inside her head saying this exact phrase.

"I see you still prefer to use twelfth century speech even when we're alone, although you know it's not really necessary."

"'Tis a habit hard to break. I have been careful with my speech for nigh unto thirty years. 'Twould be foolish on my part to make a mistake now that might cost me all if I am whisked back to the future."

"Perhaps, but it'd be nice to have someone to talk to who also came from the twenty-first century. I'm always worried about the use of my contractions when I'm dealing with running Warkworth's household, let alone letting slip a *yes* in for an *aye*."

"Have you not seen your friend Brianna of late?"

"I'm afraid not. She pregger's at the moment and Gavin refuses to allow her to travel."

"I am most certain he is also afraid she may slip through Time. I know your own husband has the same concerns."

Katherine shrugged as though her situation was not much of an annoyance. "Since you obviously don't want to discuss Killian because you're changing the subject, I'll let you escape *that* particular issue at least for now. Just know you're not getting off that easily. Instead, let's discuss why you passed out at the sight of Henry de Rune. Who is he to you?"

Ella choked on the wine she had been sipping at hearing Henry's name slip through another's lips. That he had ridden by her with no recognition had torn at her heart. Yet 'twas only natural since they had not as yet met. Seeing him had been a shock, especially knowing how her feelings for Killian had grown in the short time they had traveled together. Her face heated at the thought of their last kiss and her own admission she had feelings for him.

"Does he come this way often?" Ella asked, instead of dwelling on her feeling that she had betrayed Henry, although, in all honesty, she did not feel as upset as she thought she would. She set down her chalice, knowing she would most likely continue to choke on her wine while they discussed Henry... or Killian.

"No. We've never met before. He spent only the one night with us before he said he needed to travel to another castle close by to meet with the parents of the woman he's to marry. Warkworth was a convenient place to rest his horse. Why?"

"He is the man I crossed Time for," Ella blurted out.

"Holy shit! Are you kidding me? He's *that* man?"

"Aye," she replied, a little shocked at hearing a woman

swearing so openly. It had been some time since she had been in Katherine's company and Ella was not used to something that would have been common in their own time.

"Sorry I implied there was something between you and Killian then. I was just certain of..." her words trailed off while she rubbed her finger across her lips.

"Certain of what?"

"You called out his name while you were sleeping," she answered.

"Henry's?"

"No. Killian's."

"'Tis nothing to jest about, Katherine," Ella said sternly.

"I agree, but the way you two clung to one another while you slept only reaffirmed my belief you had found your match, Ella."

"But Henry..."

Katherine held up her hand stopping her words and Ella clamped her lips together. "Hear me out, dearest Ella. While I won't try to presume to know all the details of your story before you became lost in Time, you were indeed lost not once but twice. You told me your story, although you never specifically mentioned de Rune or your husband by name."

"'Twas best not to reveal my past," Ella interrupted before taking another sip of her wine.

Katherine gave her a soft smile before continuing. "Henry served his purpose. He found you and you fell in love with him. But you fell through Time again and lived a whole new lifetime, Ella. Maybe everything that happened with Henry, and even the man you married in order to stay safe in the twelfth-century, was in preparation for you to truly find the one man you actually came through Time for... Killian. Everything had to happen exactly as it did in order for you to find the happiness and love you clearly have found if you only let that love into your heart."

"But I have spent the last thirty years loving Henry and wanting to be reunited with him again," Ella said, even as her stomach clenched with uncertainty.

"I've no doubt that loving Henry is exactly what you have thought and felt. But I'm not blind and I know what I've seen. Don't be foolish enough to let Killian slip from your grasp, because love will find you when you least expect it and I'm pretty damn sure you already know that too."

"You have given me much to think on," Ella murmured.

Katherine stood and came over to give Ella a hug. "You know how much I love you, Ella. You've been like another mother to me. I only want you to find what I myself have found with Riorden. He was worth all the sacrifices I made so I could stay with him in this time and I'd do it all over again in a heartbeat. Now, I'll let you get some rest. I'm sure a servant will be arriving soon with your food."

After Katherine's departure, Ella continued to stare into the flames of the fire hardly seeing or even feeling the heat. A servant came and went but her meal grew cold. The wine dulled her senses. She crawled once more into bed to sleep the night away. And when she dreamed, she dreamed of a man with a Scottish brogue and blue-green eyes, her arms wrapped possessively around him as she craved his kisses and the warmth of his body to make her feel whole again.

CHAPTER 13

Killian stumbled his way down the stone stairs and into the great hall of Warkworth Castle. The remainder of his eve after he left Ella's chamber had been a restless one. Sleep had evaded him, for his thoughts constantly turned to the one woman who owned his heart. Frustration that Ella had been so moved to see her previous lover ran through his mind over and over again 'til he finally found solace in several tankards of ale. Drink may have aided him in at last finding his sleep but 'twas also the reason for his pounding head this early in the morn. He shook what lingered at the bottom of the pitcher he held and listened to the liquid slosh within. He had consumed far more than he had thought last eve.

Riorden was at the head table breaking his fast. Patrick, the youngest of the MacLaren siblings, had been Riorden's squire for several years now and silently stood behind his lord awaiting orders. Killian gave the young lad a nod before Riorden motioned for Killian to take a seat. A servant quickly set a bowl in front of him along with a piece of bread. The smell of porridge assaulted his senses causing Killian to raise his fist to his mouth. His eyes watered, even while his stomach rolled at the thought of food.

"'Twill help," Riorden offered nudging the bowl closer, "and only sleep will help you see clearly again."

"I do not think I can stomach food, Laird Riorden," he groaned, taking in the much younger man. He held nothing but respect for the knight who was once captain of Dristan of Berwyck's personal guards, especially since Riorden had aided in saving the Lady Amiria long ago.

"Suit yourself but, as my Katherine would say, 'hangovers are a bitch'. Take it from someone who knows and avoids them at all cost. You best heed my advice and eat." Riorden chuckled taking another spoonful from his own meal.

Killian poured the remainder of his ale into his cup. "Ye will not join me for a drink?" he asked taking a swig with an attempt not to grimace as the liquid slid its way down to his empty stomach. 'Twas a mistake to think additional ale might help his plight.

Riorden held up his hand. "Nay. I cannot stomach the stuff this early in the morn and as I said, I have had my fill of overindulging to last me a lifetime but you enjoy... if you can, that is."

Killian put down the pitcher wondering if he had offended his host by drinking this early in the morn. How could Killian have forgotten years ago that Riorden had been drugged by his father's widow when she put poison in his drink? The daft woman had hoped to rekindle the love she and Riorden had once held for one another, as if that would ever erase her betrayal. Her attempts had left Riorden in a daze for many months and 'twas lucky she had not killed the man.

He pulled the bowl closer and took a tentative taste of his meal. The first bite barely went down. The second was much easier. "Ye may be right about eating instead of drinking, lad," Killian said breaking off a piece of bread and dunking it into the porridge.

Laughter rumbled within Riorden's chest. "I have been known to speak a fair amount of wisdom if one cares to but listen and heed my advice."

"Ye have done well for yerself, my laird, since ye left Berwyck's service."

Riorden pushed aside his dish. "I still miss the days of old on occasion but I have no regrets. How could I, now that I have a lovely wife and a child to see to."

"And another one on the way," Killian added, "not that I should be speaking of such things but 'tis hard not tae notice yer lady's condition.

"Aye, my lady is a stubborn one and would not listen when I told her she should be in confinement until after the birth. The babe shall be called Jocelyn, after my mother. Katherine insisted and I would not gainsay her in the naming of our child. My lady insists we shall have a daughter." Riorden gave him a knowing look as though he, too, was privy to the bairn's gender.

"'Tis a wonderful way of honoring yer mother." Killian gave a wishful sigh, knowing he would never be so blessed as to have a wee bairn to call his own. "There have been many changes since ye left Berwyck," Killian continued changing the subject of women and their condition. "Now with Fletcher fancying another of those future women appearing at Berwyck's gates,

Dristan fears he will not have many knights left tae train and guard his keep."

Riorden leaned back in his chair. "Surely not everything has changed. 'Tis not every day that one has the privilege to train with the Devil's Dragon. There was always some young fool ready to take up arms to prove his worth. Now should be no exception."

"Lately, those who have thought themselves worthy have not held promise that would easily measure up tae yer standards, at least in the eyes of Laird Dristan."

"I am hard to replace," Riorden chuckled, barely containing his merriment he had obviously been missed. "But there is always a first for everything, or so Katherine reminds me on more occasions than I can count."

"Ye seem happy and I am glad for it."

"I am content only because of the love of a good woman," Riorden confided. "But what of your own story with the Lady Ella? Surely 'tis nonsense of escorting her to some man she met years ago. Who is the chap? Anyone I know?"

Killian cleared his throat. "Ye have met him."

"I have?"

"Aye, 'tis the gent who was leaving yester eve when we rode up. 'Tis the reason Ella passed out. Apparently seeing the knight got the best of her."

"But Henry de Rune is already spoken for, although he made mention of his first wife who passed away that he had never gotten over. He goes to make the final arrangements with the parents of his intended."

Killian's brows furrowed at the thought of de Rune and Ella together. He still had a hard time trying to think of her living her life all over again just to be with a man she barely knew. "And therein lays the problem, I suppose, and something Ella is certainly aware of."

"I thought perchance the two of you had come to some understanding."

"Nay... unfortunately for my sorry arse, there is nothing tae settled between us. She still insists she must needs meet the man on some country road."

Riorden scowled. "And yet Katherine made mention you stood vigil at Ella's bedside and refused to leave 'til you were assured she would be fine."

"I do not think even Ella knows what or who she really wants tae share her life," Killian said attempting to hide his disappointment. He brushed his hand across his eyes as if to clear his vision.

"You care for her, that much is obvious," Riorden surmised.

"Of course, I care for her. How could I not?" Killian groaned. "However, 'twill not do me much good if she continues tae pine away for another."

Before Riorden could reply, the Lady Katherine came into view. She stopped at the foot of the stairs gazing around her hall, a look of confusion marred her face.

She made her way to her husband, kissing his cheek. "Good morning, my love," she murmured in his ear.

Riorden took his hand and placed it on her protruding belly. "How fare thee this morn, my lady?"

"We are both fine, my lord, but where's Ella? I expected her to be here having breakfast since she wasn't in her chamber," she asked looking around again apparently on the off chance she had missed her. "Patrick... you rise earlier than any of us. Have you seen Lady Ella?"

"Nay, my lady. I have not seen her this morn," Patrick replied.

"Riorden?" Katherine asked turning toward her husband.

"I have not seen her as yet and I have been here for some time." Riorden answered before turning to Killian. "Have you had speech with your lady this morn?"

"Nay, I have not. Where could she be?" Killian stood ready to search the castle stone by stone if he must.

"Let's not panic," Katherine said taking her seat. "I'm sure she's close by and wouldn't leave the castle grounds."

"I wouldnae be so certain of that, Lady Katherine. Ella's a stubborn woman when she has an idea in her head. If she wanted tae leave the castle, I have no doubt she would find a way."

"We take no chances with the lady's safety given she took flight from Berwyck to escape capture," Riorden replied before calling out to one of his knights. "Caldwell!"

Leaving his place at one of the tables and working his way to the front of the hall, Caldwell gave a low bow. "Aye, my lord?"

"Search the grounds for the Lady Ella and report back while we organize a search of the keep."

"'Twill be done, my lord," Caldwell answered before running off to do his lord's bidding.

Killian began making his way to the stairs. "I shall search her room and floor tae see if she is about."

"Finish your meal, Killian, while we check with the servants to see if they have seen her," Riorden urged as he waved his hand at Killian's vacated chair.

"Nay. I cannae rest 'til she is found and I know she is safe," Killian replied taking the steps two at a time.

Upon reaching the floor where Ella's chamber resided, he

first went to Lady Katherine's solar but found the room empty except a servant tending the fire. Leaving the room, he passed a garderobe and decided to check there as well. He swung open the door with nary a knock, not caring if he would embarrass Ella if she were about her private business. Still, the room was as vacant as Lady Katherine's solar.

He began to panic and ran the rest of the way down the passageway. He gave the briefest of knocks before entering Ella's room. His eyes scanned the interior and his brows furrowed. Nothing appeared out of place 'til he noticed the cloak she had worn when the traveled was nowhere to be seen. He swore. How could the woman be stupid enough to leave the castle without him or at the very least a guard for her protection?

He had just closed the door wondering where Ella could have gone when he heard his name being yelled from down below. He ran to the stairs to return to the hall, hoping upon hope that nothing had happened to Ella.

Hearing Katherine and Riorden in a heated conversation caused Killian to halt his hurried stride across the chamber.

"Nay, I will not hear of it, you stubborn woman," Riorden yelled. "You shall not leave this castle, let alone its grounds, to go traipsing about the countryside in your condition!"

"Just because I'm pregnant doesn't mean I'm an invalid, Riorden," Katherine fumed with hands upon her hips. "Besides you can hold my hand the entire time if you're afraid of losing me."

"You are going to be the death of me, my love," Riorden sighed before yanking her into his arms and holding her within his embrace.

"No I won't and you *will* let me accompany you," she

answered reaching up on her toes to place a kiss upon his cheek, "because you love me."

Before Riorden could answer, Killian interrupted them. "Do ye have some news of Ella?" he asked.

Riorden shook his head. "Nay, not from any of the guards."

Confused, Killian looked between the pair. "Then why are ye calling me as though ye have found her?"

Katherine turned putting her arm around her husband's waist before giving Killian a bright smile. "I have a feeling I know where she's gone."

CHAPTER 14

Ella pulled at the small boat she had kept hidden in the bushes for years. She had been this way on more than one occasion, although it had been some time since she had been on a pilgrimage to say her prayers. In her future life, she had never been one to go to Mass on a daily basis. In reality, she rarely went into a church, although she still believed in a higher being. But living in the twelfth-century changes a person and attending Mass every morning had become a normal occurrence when she had lived with her husband. If she had not been present during Mass, her people would have thought this odd since she was the lady of Hull.

As she pushed the boat into the water, she held on tight to the edge before jumping inside and taking up the oar. 'Twas just a short trip across the waterway to the other side and yet the current was strong on the Coquet River. She would need all her strength just to steer the boat and keep it true to her course.

Killian would know by now she had left the safety of the

keep and would be furious with her. But she needed this time unto herself to get her thoughts together on where her life would now lead her. She would beg his forgiveness in the hope he would understand her plight and the turmoil her heart was in.

Leaving the castle grounds unnoticed had been no small feat. 'Twas as though God had given her a sign when a timely distraction caused one of the guards to leave his post near the postern gate. This allowed Ella to quickly slip through without anyone's notice. She had been relieved for the opportunity presented to her. She was in no mood to deal with Killian's anger, nor Katherine's pleading to use their chapel instead of where she was now headed.

Making it across the river, the boat bumped into the shore and Ella jumped out narrowly missing her step upon the bank. Her balance faltered and she almost fell backwards into the water. Yet, she righted herself in time and once more tugged the boat up onto the shore. Taking a rope anchored to a bolt, she tied her small vessel to a nearby tree. No sense in taking chances her one way to return to the other side of the river would somehow find its way back into the water to float away and leave her stranded.

She grabbed a bunch of wildflowers she had quickly gathered on her frantic flight from Warkworth before making her way through the trees. She knew this path well and memories of when she had pulled a half-drowned woman from the river flooded her mind. She had been so afraid the poor lady would not last the night and yet she had lived. 'Twas the day her friendship with Katherine had begun… two women stranded in time, although Ella had not shared such knowledge with Katherine. Both women should have never found their way to twelfth-century England in the first place, and yet here they were, each living their lives as though they had always belonged here.

Ella found the entrance to what Katherine had said in the future was called the Hermitage. As far as Ella was concerned, the place was little more than a cave. Yet someone had already made what she had considered an altar for her prayers and a place to light a fire to take the chill from the place. She knelt down by the hearth and saw someone had been there at some point since her last visit given the amount of wood and kindling located in a nearby basket. She found the flint she had kept there and began working on a fire. Before long, she had an adequate blaze going. She took off her cloak, grabbed the bouquet, and then placed it on the altar. Kneeling, she began to pray.

With an earnest heart, Ella prayed for her family whom she had not seen in many years. Did they still search for her or was Time fickle and to them mayhap they had only seen her but yesterday? She begged for their forgiveness for wanting to stay in this place and time so that she, too, could find love. She begged for the forgiveness of her sins, especially in failing her son.

Faramond... A mother's love ran deep and yet how would she ever learn to forgive her son's betrayal? How could she have failed so horribly in his upbringing that her son cared more for his position and the gold in his coffers than he cared about the woman who gave him life?

Simon... Ella said a prayer for the man who saved her from uncertain doom in the twelfth-century. She supposed she did him wrong far worse than any of her other sins, marrying him while staying loyal in her love to another man.

She frowned at the memory of Simon answering a summons

from the king and word reaching her that her husband was accused of treason. Confused, she turned to her grown son to find the cause for the king's belief that Simon would have done such an offense. Yet, by the time Faramond reached London, 'twas too late. He returned with his father's body to bury in the family cemetery. Simon was barely in the ground before she confessed her origins to her son, who threw her out of his life as though he was tossing out the refuse. She shuddered and prayed for Simon to forgive her.

Henry... she had loved him for so very long, and had dreamed of returning to his side for thirty years. Was it really just yester eve that their paths had crossed only for him to not have even the slightest idea of what they would one day mean to one another? She prayed for him to forgive her for all that would never be.

Killian... Within one heartbeat her feelings had changed so much so that she was now in love with another man other than Henry. Aye, she loved Killian, may God above forgive her for that too. She had spent so many years traveling near and far just to pass time 'til she could be reunited with the one man she had thought she had crossed time for. How ironic was it that she was on the threshold of meeting him when she finally faced the truth that the man she crossed Time for had been waiting at Berwyck all along?

She was a fool because only a person who was daft in the head would take so long to discover the man she truly loved with every breath she took had been right in front of her every single time she wandered to Berwyck's gates. She prayed that Killian, too, would forgive her for being blind to all the wasted years they could have shared together if only she had opened her eyes to see the possibilities loving him would offer.

She prayed for strength. She prayed for the safety of those she loved, both in her past life and those in her present. She prayed for…

Ella raised her head and peered into the darkness beyond the light of the walls surrounding her. Something was out of place and yet she was unsure what noise had alerted her enough to disturb her vigilant prayers.

She held her breath as a dark shape took the unmistakable form of a man at the entrance. She smiled, knowing Killian had found her. She stood, ready to welcome him and finally profess the love she felt for him in her heart. Yet her face fell when the man came into the light of the room and her heart faltered at what fate now had in store for her.

"Hello, mother," Faramond sneered. "'Tis time for you to come home."

He stepped forward with rope in hand, even as Ella let out a bloodcurdling scream. Yet, she knew no one would hear her for none knew her whereabouts. Faramond laughed causing Ella to feel faint knowing she was now in his hands. May God above help Killian find her, for he was the only one who could save her now.

CHAPTER 15

Faramond struggled getting his mother out of the boat and onto his horse. 'Twas sheer luck he had come across her figure in the early morn as she scurried from the nearby castle. He had followed her at some distance to watch where she might be headed without escort. When she pulled a boat out of some bushes and made her way across the river, he had backtracked and tossed a coin to a fisherman who ferried him across the water. Following her footsteps had been easy enough since she did nothing to hide her tracks.

"Let me go, son," Ella declared, her voice sharp. "There is nothing you can gain by taking me hostage and returning me to Hull."

"On the contrary, mother," he answered as he touched his heels to the side of his horse putting the steed into a canter. "The king has plans for you and if I can deliver you, he has promised to reward me."

"The king wants me at court? I hardly see what His Majesty would want with an old woman."

Faramond laughed. "He does not want *you* for himself, madam. King Henry has made an arrangement of marriage for you. I understand 'twill be a contract that will earn him a great advantage and will serve him greatly."

"M-marriage? T-to whom?" she stuttered. She swayed in the saddle and he made a grab for her before she fell and he would have to go through all his efforts to get her back on his horse.

"Does it matter? 'Tis of no import to me whom you are to wed. Suffice to say your king demanded I return you to Hull. Once we return home, I shall send a runner to London to inform him that you have willingly agreed to his wishes."

"I have agreed to nothing!" she fumed. "How dare you treat me thusly? I am your mother and deserve your respect."

"You deserve nothing, witch! Do you honestly think I have easily forgotten your crazy talk of being from the future? Do you think I have forgiven you?"

"You are still my son," she yelled, causing the birds in the treetops to take flight.

"Then as your son, I am also lord of Hull and you shall obey me and the king's directives as to your future."

"You cannot do this to me, Faramond. Please, I love another."

He pulled on the reins of his horse and tugged on the ropes 'til his dame faced him. "Think you I care who you love? Love is for fools. Coins and obedience to the crown are all that matters. My reward will be great and I will finally be able to claim my heritance that has been denied me."

"Denied you. You are the rightful heir to Hull," she cried out.

"How can the king deny you the right to be lord of your own castle?"

Faramond gave a sarcastic laugh. "Aye… how could you have known, since my father was accused of being a traitor and plotted against King Henry, that my title would be stripped from me? How could I have known when I tossed you from the grounds that I would actually need you someday to claim my lands?"

"That is ridiculous. Your father was no traitor."

"And I attempted to argue the point but there was proof such was the case. The only way I could reclaim my inheritance was to return you to Hull. Your marriage was arranged. My only problem was I could not locate you. Now that I have, everything will fall into place. Your new husband will send an escort fit for a lady of your station and you will be married before the king. Afterwards you shall travel to your new home in Spain—"

"Spain?" his mother cried out.

"—thus ensuring my fortune and good name are restored. If God grants me one wish, 'twill be to never set eyes upon your evil face again." He flicked the reins and put his horse back into motion.

"I cannot marry someone I do not love, Faramond," she whispered frantically, wondering how she would ever survive in a place so foreign and where she did not even speak the language. "Please… do not do this to me."

"You will obey me and your king."

"Tell them I am dead or you could not find me. Surely you can do at least this much for the woman who gave you life?"

"You will obey me," he repeated. "Now shut your trap lest you wish to be gagged. I have no issue performing such a service if 'twill ensure your silence."

His mother clamped her lips tight and refused to look upon him, not that he cared. Faramond's thoughts lingered upon the riches that would now come his way once his troublesome mother was no longer in his care. She did not need to know he was the one who anonymously accused his father of being a traitor. Faramond never thought that throwing his mother from Hull's gates would threaten his plan to gain full ownership of Hull. He would not be such a fool again!

CHAPTER 16

Killian raced Mystic through the village alongside Lord Riorden and his knight, Caldwell. Lady Katherine had protested against staying behind but in the end, her husband would not see her, nor the babe, possibly injured by riding upon a horse. Instead, Katherine had reminded Riorden of the location of the Hermitage and approximately where they would need to cross the river to find it.

They slowed their steeds when they reached the bank of the river and, before long, they were rowing their way across, pulling their boat onto the other side of the shore and making their way through the foliage. The mouth of a cave in the rock face loomed before them.

Riorden led the way into the darkness.

"How is it that I have lived here for many a year and have never known such a place existed?" Caldwell muttered.

"I did not wish to draw attention to the place. Even I never knew this place was here and I grew up at Warkworth," Riorden said as he continued onward.

Killian muttered a curse. "I think we are wasting our time. How would Ella get herself across the river?" he asked rubbing his arms. "It took a fair amount of strength tae row the boat myself, never mind she be a small woman."

Riorden laughed. "You should learn, *mon ami*, never to underestimate what drives a woman to do anything once she has her mind set to any particular task."

"But how would she know this place even existed?" Caldwell inquired.

"She has never divulged such information to me but, needless to say, she has come to this Hermitage for many years to say her prayers. Katherine showed it to me after she returned to Warkwork, although I refused to allow her to come here on her own."

"With good reason, no doubt," Caldwell stated.

"There is a light up ahead. Mayhap we have found the lady after all." Killian rushed forward, ready to give his lady a sound tongue lashing for her foolishness.

He stumbled to a sudden halt, causing Riorden and Caldwell to almost bump into him. The chamber was vacant and yet a fire was still lit and warmed the room. Given the overturned stool and the marks upon the dirt beneath their feet, a scuffled had occurred.

Riorden went to the altar and picked up the fresh bouquet of flowers, even while Killian picked up Ella's discarded cloak from the floor. He held her garment up to his nose and could smell the sweet fragrance of the woman he had come to love. "She was here."

"Aye," Riorden declared, "but obviously she is no longer

and, from the look of things, the lady did not leave on her own accord."

"Faramond," Killian hissed.

"You are sure?" Riorden asked.

"Who else would take her," Killian growled in anger. "I swear, if her son has harmed her in anyway, I shall take great pleasure in killing him."

Quickly dousing the fire, they ran to the boat and were once more rowing their way across the river. Killian's nerves were stretched to their limit for it seemed as if it took a lifetime to make their way to the other bank.

Riorden disembarked and made his way to a fisherman who was just leaving the dock with a basket of fish.

"Are you certain?" Riorden inquired slapping his gloves against his leg.

"Aye, milord, I took the gent across the way," he said pointing to the other side of the river.

"Was he from the village?" Killian asked, hoping such would be the case but he had a feeling in his gut he already knew the answer.

"Nay, sir, 'e be a stranger to me. Said 'e be lookin' for his mother, 'e did. Saw no reason to not 'elp the gent out," he said wringing his hands. "Did I do somethin' wrong, milord?"

"Nay. You are not at fault." Riorden proclaimed. He took a coin from the pouch at his belt and tossed it to the man. "For your troubles."

"Thank ye, milord," the man bobbed before taking off towards the village.

The three men made their way to their horses. Mounting up, Killian put on his gloves. "I make for Hull," he announced."

Riorden gave Beast a pat upon his neck while donning his own gauntlets. "You need knights to watch your back."

"Nay, I will travel faster alone."

"Do not be a fool, Killian," Riorden ordered. "You are not prepared and have nothing with you to sustain your travels, let alone a rescue."

"I have managed before with much less," he proclaimed.

Riorden's brow rose as he took in Killian's meager possessions. "You have your horse and your cloak. How much less could you survive with?"

"'Tis enough. Besides, I have trained with the Devil's Dragon. Surely there is no need tae tell ye, of all people, that I can survive."

Riorden muttered beneath his breath. "Dristan *and* Amiria will both have my head if something befalls you. At least take Caldwell with you. He will not slow you down and I trust him."

Killian gazed at both men, briefly contemplating Riorden's offer. "Nay, but I give ye my thanks for the offer. I still feel I will be better off traveling on my own. No offense, Caldwell."

Caldwell threw up his hands. "None taken but I think you are making a mistake. There is safety in numbers."

"I will return *with* the Lady Ella and for our second steed," Killian said giving them a look of what he hoped was confidence.

Riorden nodded. "See that you do. I do not relish having to explain to my Katherine that you failed in your quest to rescue her friend because you refused our extra help. You have a long ride ahead of you, *mon ami*."

With a jaunty salute, Killian kicked Mystic into motion. With a small measure of luck, he just might catch up with his lady before they reach Hull. He had a gut wrenching feeling no matter what happened he would be spending a considerable amount of time scouting out the castle layout for him to find a way to rescue his lady.

CHAPTER 17

They traveled south in relative silence. Her son made no efforts to communicate with her. On one hand, Ella was glad for it, for what was there really to say to a man who had become all but a complete stranger to her? On the other, she mourned the days when her son had been young and looked to her for guidance. Those days were obviously long since gone. Faramond had returned from his fostering in disgrace, angry and bitter, and Simon had been furious with the way he had behaved. She had thought time would heal the wounds, but instead Simon had died and she had been exiled.

She had been such a fool to confess her origins to Faramond all those years ago in an effort for him to understand how lost she had felt at the time of his father's passing.

Simon of Hull had been a handsome man with black curly hair and light blue eyes. She studied her son's profile from lowered lashes. A modern phrase flitted across her mind. The apple had not fallen far from the tree as far as her son was concerned. Faramond was almost an exact replica of her late husband. She could have been looking in a mirror of her husband's younger self. As they neared the village of Hull, her past life flashed across her mind's eye, and, with those images, she wiped away an unexpected tear. She tried to count the number of years it had been since she last stepped foot in a place she had called home. 'Twas at least ten when she made the mistake of getting too close to Hull, although it made no difference now. She looked ahead at the thriving river port.

A sob almost escaped her lips and she forced her emotions to recede back into the deepest place within her. She had locked such tormenting memories away and kept them hidden from any who made any attempt to pry into her life. Even those who had become close to her did not truly know of the extent of her exile. She would be damned if she would give Faramond the satisfaction of knowing how his treatment of her was affecting her.

As though he knew her thoughts had momentarily settled upon him, her son pulled sharply on the reins of the horse, stopping the beast before they entered the village. He was not even gentle with an animal that had carried him far in his travels. Ella did not expect her own treatment to be any better, considering she had been taken against her will. Her raw wrists where the rope had cut into them ensuring her captivity were witness to his cruelty.

"You will obey me and remember your place in *my* household," Faramond ordered with a smug look as he stared at her tied hands. 'Twas as though he gained confidence in his ability to keep her under his control. Taking a dirk from his belt, he slit the abrasive cords that had bound her. Ella rubbed at her mistreated limbs. "Do you understand me, mother?"

"I am perfectly capable of hearing you, son," Ella replied, a hint of defiance all but dripping from her words.

"You shall show me respect at all times, lest you wish to be bound again or put into the dungeon."

"And if you wish to remain in the good graces of your people, you shall do the same in my case. I am certain there will be several amongst those living within Hull who shall remember I was once mistress here," Ella stated, watching for any sign of the young man she had once proudly called her son. But the look he gave her told her she should not hold her breath waiting for a miracle he would change. Apparently, greed had become Faramond's master and the Devil owned a part of his soul for him to treat his own flesh and blood in such a manner.

He opened and closed his mouth several times before he answered her with clenched teeth. "'Twill be your choice how you are treated while you remain in my hall."

"Technically, I believe 'tis *my* hall," she laughed to further annoy him.

Faramond's face turned purple with rage. "You defy me even at my own gates?" he snarled.

"You have not given me any indication that there is still some love left in your heart for me. 'Til you do so, you are nothing to me and certainly nary my son," she exclaimed raising her chin to drive her point home. "Now let us see how you have taken care of Hull in my absence. This should prove very interesting."

Faramond gave a growl of outrage before turning in the saddle and slapping the reins against his horse. 'Twas as though the steed knew it should make haste lest it anger his master and feel the lash against his flesh.

They made good time through the village before coming

toward the river's edge. There in the distance was her home, but 'twas not the home she remembered. Her home had been a lovely keep rising three stories some distance from the edge of the river and giving her a delightful view of the surrounding countryside. Faramond had been busy, for how long Ella could not say. The beginnings of a battlement wall were progressing, and she could only ponder what other developments had changed her castle since she had last resided within its protective walls.

They entered the courtyard and she saw the sturdy door and entryway into the keep. Ella closed her eyes. Once again, images worth a full lifetime raced in front of her as though she could even now see her son playing in the courtyard with a wooden sword made by his father.

The last time she had seen Simon had been on the day he was to travel to London. Opening her eyes, her gaze once more landed upon the keep. She had stood on those very same steps while her husband bade her farewell. How was she to know 'twould be the last time she would see him alive? Would she have asked him to forgive her for never truly loving him the way he deserved to be loved if she had known? How many times in their past had she caught his gaze, making her feel guilty she was incapable of loving Simon as much as she had loved Henry?

Simon had been so in love with her he turned a blind eye to all her faults and still cared for her to the best of his ability. Poor Simon... he deserved so much better than a woman who settled into a life with him so he could provide her a safe haven to live.

She gave a heavy sigh. When Simon's body had been returned to Hull by her son, Faramond would not give her any details of how Simon had died. Ella had been devastated to see his body wrapped in linens in the back of a lowly wagon. She had begged Faramond to tell her of his death but he had refused, stating the how and why of it did not matter. But the manner of his death did matter, at least to her, not that her son offered her any form of solace in her time of grief. She may not have been in love with Simon but that did not mean she did not care for the man.

'Twas still odd after all these years that Faramond would not divulge such information to his own mother. Mayhap there was more to the story of this supposed betrayal Simon committed to the crown than Faramond had told her. That had been the day she had confessed her origins to her son. She never expected Faramond to disown his own mother and kick her off the estate with her dead husband barely into his grave. Even after all these years, she swore her knees and palms still hurt from the stones she had landed upon when she had fallen.

"By the Blessed Saints, 'tis Lady Ella returned to us," a woman's voice called out.

Ella knew that tone. How could she not? Her gaze swept the courtyard before they fell upon one of the ladies who had attended her all those years ago. A small smile of recognition escaped Ella's lips remembering the kindness this woman had always extended her, especially in those first days when she felt so out of place… and time.

"Isabel. How good it is to see you after all these years," Ella beamed, extending her hands in friendship. The woman lessened the distance between them and grasped her outstretched limbs.

"You have been missed, my lady," Isabel murmured, keeping her voice low. She cast a hesitant look upon Faramond whose contempt registered on his visage 'til he called for a stable lad to take his horse.

Taking off his leather gloves, he slapped them upon his thighs. "I will see you at the evening meal, mother," he declared before dismissing them and taking his leave.

Ella shivered and shook her head, as though such an act could erase the disappointment overwhelming her at her son's behavior.

"I have much to tell you, my lady," Isabel said, once they were alone in the courtyard.

"Just Ella," she said with one shred of hope she could remain an ordinary woman and not one who bore a lofty title as mistress of a keep. Isabel's next words confirmed she would not be given that mercy.

"I would not dare to call you by your given name, Lady Ella."

She linked her arm through Isabel's. "Then we shall remain on a first name basis while we are alone behind the closed doors of my chamber. I could use a friend to have speech with. I assume I am to have my old rooms?"

"I am sure your son will see to the matter."

A snort slipped through Ella's lips. "I doubt he will give me much thought now that he has returned me to Hull. But let us see where I can rest my head and perchance clean up from my travels."

They entered the keep and Ella stumbled as memories assaulted her mind yet again. Closing her eyes, she conjured up the image of Killian, wondering if, even at this very moment, he was searching for her. She gave a heavy sigh and began to wonder if her life would ever be simple again.

CHAPTER 18

Killian made his way through the village before peeking around a pole by a vegetable stall. He observed Ella strolling through the market square in the company of another woman. 'Twas the moment he had been waiting for and he was glad to see she had not been thrown into a dungeon. Such a location would make releasing her from her current situation a far more difficult quest.

The two women appeared on friendly terms, if their laughter was any indication as to their relationship. His scowl deepened while he watched the merriment between to the two ladies. What was there to jest about, given her predicament? One would think from looking at them that they did not have a care in the world. Such a thought quickly disappeared when his lady looked over her shoulder. Even over the distance separating them, Killian could see Ella's smile fade into a grim line of discontent. She was not pleased, nor could he blame her.

His attention moved to the two guards who were following

directly behind her. Their close proximity to his lady would not leave him much of an opportunity to have a private word with her. They were heavily armed and yet Killian had no doubt he could best either of them if the matter arose. *Bloody hell! How in heaven's name will I rescue, Ella?* he mused before scratching at his beard while he puzzled over their dilemma.

Their group began strolling on to the next stall and Killian continued to watch their progress from his place of concealment. His thoughts wandered over the past several days. He had been relieved when he first espied Hull and the place Ella had once called her home. Although located next to the river, there were no battlement walls to impede his entrance into the estate, although 'twas not hard to miss the beginnings of one being constructed. But 'twould take many a year before the keep was surrounded in a wall of protection for those who would dwell within the castle. Killian prayed he and Ella would be long gone from this place by then.

Shaking his head, he was abruptly taken out of his musings when he noticed the woman next to Ella move across the village to inspect a stall not far from him. He prayed he could trust the woman to get a message to Ella, given what he had seen but moments before. Surely, he knew Ella well enough to be able to read the signs that her companion was not in cahoots with her son's devious plans.

Retracing his steps behind the back of the stalls, he reached the end of the row and waited for the lady to make her way nearer before he made his presence known. Stepping through the draped linen at the back of the stall, he hopefully appeared as though he was just another potential buyer or mayhap the seller.

"Ye be friends with the Lady Ella," he murmured, for her

ears alone. He mentally cursed as he listened to his accent, which would certainly give these Englishmen reason to wonder what a Scot was doing so far south and out of his element.

The woman had been in the process of sniffing a piece of fruit. Her gaze went to him and her eyes widened before she quickly scanned the area. Luckily, she was not being watched as closely as her mistress. "My name is Isabel. Are you perchance Killian?" she asked, reaching for his wrist as though to hold him in place.

Killian smiled, knowing his lady had spoken of him. "Aye, and 'tis pleasing tae my ears tae learn ye have knowledge of me."

"You are all she speaks of," the woman confessed, giving Killian a warm feeling in the pit of his belly.

"Is my lady well?"

"As well as can be expected, I suppose, although her son has threatened to toss her into the keep's pit on more than one occasion."

He grimaced thinking of the one located in the depths of Berwyck. "Pits... they are a nasty place tae keep a prisoner."

"Aye, they are, and the one located at Hull is especially vile, considering the close proximity to the river," she replied. She continued her assessment of him. "You are here to rescue her?"

"Why else would I be this far south?"

"You must do so, then, with all haste. A runner has been sent to London and I have no doubt her intended husband will travel to Hull to collect his bride. 'Twill make no difference to him whether she is willing to marry him or not."

A low snarl passed Killian's lips. "I would willingly die to save Ella from such a fate."

"Let us hope 'twill not come down to you giving up your life for hers." Her name was called by one of the guards and she held up a finger to indicate she was almost done. "I must leave. Do you have a message for my lady?"

Killian opened the pouch at his side and pulled out his mother's ring. "Give this to her and let her know she shall be free as soon as I can figure out how to earn her release."

"I shall tell her your message." She took the ring and tucked it inside her cloak before she turned to take her leave.

"Lady Isabel…"

The woman smiled. "I am a simple woman, Killian, and certainly hold no title. Isabel will do. You have more to your message?"

Killian cleared his throat for Isabel's comment sounded so like Ella that the resemblance was startling. "Aye… tell my lady tae be well and rest easy knowing I am near. I willnae fail her again."

Isabel nodded and quickly left making her way back to Ella's side. While their party began to make their way toward the keep, Isabel whispered in Ella's ear. Ella, in turn, almost fell face forward from what Killian assumed was Isabel telling her his message. She halted their progress and he could hear her informing the guards she had a pebble in her shoe. With Isabel's assistance, Ella removed her shoe but as she went to put it back on, she looked across the market.

Their eyes met and Killian felt a zing of emotions while he held her gaze. Ella placed her hand over her heart. He nodded and returned her loving gesture before the spell was broken by one of her guards telling her to hurry. She gave one last look upon him before she continued her stride back to the keep.

Killian had watched her 'til she disappeared from sight. His mind going in a hundred directions, he could only ponder what he could do next to ensure his lady's freedom.

CHAPTER 19

Shrieks of outrage poured forth from Ella's lips. Yet for all her screaming, her son's guardsman continued to force her down the steep steps towards the dark cellars below. She kicked. She bit him. She swung her fists hitting him on any part of his body she could reach but this only caused the knight to hold her even tighter. He began to threaten her even while she heard her son chuckling behind them on the stairs.

"You shall not harm one hair upon her head lest you wish to answer to me," Faramond warned, surprising Ella that he cared enough to actually come to her defense. "Set her down."

"Aye, my lord."

Ella was swung down from the knight's shoulder. She was about to offer her thanks to her son for coming to his senses but his words dispelled anything further thoughts from coming to her lips.

"I believe 'twould be more satisfying to lock you away myself. If you will not behave, I will then be more than happy to see you gagged and bound," he jeered. He nodded towards his man "Get below and see that her cell is opened."

Ella took a swing at her son but missed as he jerked aside. "You bas—"

Her words were cut off when Faramond caught her about the waist. "I do not believe my birth is an issue here, mother." With little thought, he picked her up to swing her over his shoulder like a sack of grain and continued carrying her down into the dim and musty cellars.

"Damn you, let me down, Faramond," she bellowed at the top of her lungs, while pounding on his back.

"Nay, I shall not. I warned you to behave yourself and yet you still defied me," he growled out.

Shoved into a cell, she stumbled once more and fell upon a straw matt laid out on the filthy floor. A puff of dust went airborne when her backside made contact with what was considered a bed. Faramond slammed the iron door shut before she could scurry forward to stop him. Turning the key, he locked her in her prison cell. She quickly made her way to the bars to give them a shake, as though by some miracle they would open because she willed it.

"Let me out this instant!" she fumed, shaking the bars once more to no avail.

Faramond chuckled. "I should have put you here the instant we reached Hull. Be thankful you are at least not residing in our pit."

She tried again to reach some compassion in her son. "You have no reason to place me here. I am your mother and have done nothing wrong." Her plea was apparently not heard.

Faramond moved forward 'til they were practically nose-to-nose through the iron bars. One of them had the freedom to leave the area. One obviously did not. "Who gave you permission to leave the keep in order to go to the village?"

With one last shove at the unforgiving bars, Ella moved away from the door. If she must be a prisoner, then so be it, but she would never again consider this uncaring man before her as her son. "You did not gainsay me when I said I wished to go."

"I told you no."

"Nay, you did not. You said to go to my chamber. I declined to listen to you and instead went to enjoy what I could of the day."

Faramond paced back and forth in the small outer area of the dungeon. "You never did listen, even while I was a young lad."

Ella frowned, hearing something in his voice that caused her to pause. "What are you talking about? I was always there for you when I could be. 'Twas not my fault that it was the custom to send you off to squire with another lord. Your father thought he was doing what was best for you." Her voice was soft and she began to realize how much her son hated both his parents for what happened to him.

"Bah! You could have ordered father to squire me himself."

"No one ordered your father to do anything if he did not wish it. You would have known this yourself if you paid attention when you were returned to us in disgrace. But nay… your only thought was of the riches that were lost to you."

"How did you—"

"What? You did not think your father and I had speech about your deeds while you were away? We knew everything you did, including impregnating your lord's daughter."

"You have no idea what that man did to me once I arrived in his house. The daily beatings were nothing compared to what he did behind closed doors."

A gasp escaped her as she understood the underlying meaning at what had happened in her son's past. "Faramond... I am sorry for whatever he—"

"Do not speak of *it* ever, mother," he shouted while his fists shook with rage. "You lost that right years ago when you sent me to squire with a man who was anything but knightly."

Faramond's face contorted in anger and Ella could only surmise what memories he was reliving. "Now that I can guess what the man did to you, was this your way of getting back at him... through his innocent child?"

He chuckled and his lips curled upward with an evil leer. "Such may have been the case at first but then I could see the benefit of such a union. 'Twas not my fault she refused me when I offered to wed with her."

"You were both but children..." Ella answered while further memories of her son's return invaded her mind.

"...and marriages were arranged by people even younger than we were, so what was the difference?" Faramond said finishing her sentence.

"Perchance if you had not bedded the girl, her parents would have accepted your offer. But you were always rash when it came to deciding how you must live your life."

"At least I offered for her. I was not even her first," he bellowed.

Ella shook her head. "Do you think that mattered in the eyes of her parents? Does your offer change anything when their only child killed herself instead of accepting her fate that you impregnated her? Of course, they blamed you." Ella made the sign of the cross offering a quick prayer for the dead girl's soul.

"You talk too much." Faramond's fist landed upon the bars of her cage before he stepped back.

"'The truth sometimes hurts, does it not, my son?" Ella's voice cracked in grief. She made her way to a small stool located in the corner of her cell. Taking hold of it, she brought it forward and sat. Folding her hands on her lap she stared at her son.

"'Tis not my fault she took her life! 'Twas her choice, not mine."

"Where did I go wrong in raising you?" Ella whispered before heaving a heavy sigh. "If only I could change whatever sin you feel I did to you."

"Enough of this foolishness. I will no longer cater to your whims. I will not let you have your freedom of the estate or spend years of my life searching for you if you were to escape yet again. Now you shall go nowhere except to the altar to speak your vows once your betrothed arrives."

He left her without even one last glance in her direction. Tears slid down Ella's cheeks. "If I could turn back the hands of time, mayhap I would try to convince Simon to let Faramond stay with us. I wonder if that would have made any kind of difference in the man my son has become."

'Twas no use pondering an event that would never happen. There were only two outcomes to her situation that Ella could foresee... either her groom would appear taking her to Spain to live out the rest of her days or Killian would somehow manage to rescue her from this dungeon. She might as well get ready to say her vows for she was losing hope she would ever see Killian again.

Killian was at his wits end. With no way to get word to Ella, he was left waiting outside the keep, wondering as to her fate. They were losing precious time if he was to keep his vow to reunite Ella with the man she loved.

His gut wrenched at the thought of Ella with anyone else but him. If he could but earn her release from her son's clutches, he would profess his love and be damned to the consequences. He knew within his soul she cared for him. He just needed to hear the words pour from her lovely mouth and then she could release him from a vow he never should have made in the first place. He was such a fool!

He tossed a coin to the merchant and took the wedge of cheese he had purchased. Bread and cheese made a simple way to break ones fast. He gave a wistful sigh as he longed to return to Berwyck's hall and the bounty found at its tables.

Sauntering along the River Hull, he pondered his fate that was tied to a woman originally not from this time. He was aware there had been other women who had come before her to Berwyck's gates, whether they had done so willingly or not. But he never thought he would find himself falling in love with one of them. And yet Ella had spent almost as much time as an adult here in the past as she had in her future life, or so she had told him.

He could not imagine having to live your life all over again. Living in the present was enough for him. He was a simple man and had no desire to seek the fame and glory that the younger knights who came to Berwyck claimed. Having Ella to love would be enough but would *he* ever be enough for Ella? He had no hall to call his own. Would living at Berwyck satisfy a woman who previously had an entire estate where she had been its mistress?

Looking up, Killian realized he had ventured further along the riverbank than he had originally intended. As he turned, he saw Ella's attendant making her way toward him in a hurried stride.

"Sir Killian, at last I have found you," she said in a rush, while attempting to catch her breath.

"Is something wrong, Mistress Isabel? Is Ella unwell?" he asked, afraid to hear her answer.

"I must not tarry. I do not wish to be missed and call attention to myself, or you, for that matter. As far as anyone is concerned, no one knows about you and we must needs keep it that way."

Killian took her elbow to steady her. "Then tell me your news so I may help as I can."

"My lady has been placed in the keeps dungeon. But—"

"I shall kill him," Killian hissed cutting off her words. His fists clenched, as did his jaw while thoughts of Ella wallowing in some filthy dungeon filled him with rage.

"There is no time for that. I have a plan. Do you know where Meaux Abbey is located?"

"Nay, but I am certain I can find it if you but give me general directions," he answered.

Isabel nodded before taking his arm as they began to walk. "This is what we need to do…"

Killian listened to Isabel's plan and thought it had merit. As they parted, a small measure of hope filled Killian's heart that he would soon see Ella again.

CHAPTER 20

Ella's whispered words were cut off when an unexpected groan escaped her lips. Reaching down, she rubbed at her knees, having lost count of the hours when she had placed herself upon the stone floor to say her prayers. Prayers for Killian to find her. Prayers for her own sorry self that she may gain a measure of courage in the event a rescue would not come to pass. Prayers for her son, for despite his treatment of her, he was still her flesh and blood and she still held out some small measure of hope that there was some bit of goodness left in his heart.

Her vision blurred and she rubbed at her tender eyes. She could tell they were puffy from the tears she had shed, and she began to wonder where the strong-willed woman from years past had gone. Her loud sigh echoed off the walls, almost confirming her worse fears. *This* was the reason she had evaded her son and kept herself hidden for so long from his attempts to find her. All her efforts had been in vain. Everything had gone up in smoke in one bit of ill-fated luck. She now found herself in a situation far more disheartening than falling through time not once but twice.

Ella's heart shattered from the injustice of it all. *How much more was one woman supposed to endure?* she mused silently, while raising her eyes to the heavens as if God had not forsaken her. Despair consumed Ella. She felt as though she was broken and did not know how she could fix what she had no control over.

She at last took a grim look at what she could see of her surroundings. Her prison cell was just that. There were no windows to see the time of day, although she presumed night had fallen. Her sense of smell was heightened only because of the dampness seeping into her bones as she shivered from the cold. 'Twas another reminder that the stones around her hid from view the fact the keep was situated up against the River Hull. The candle her son had left for her was almost spent. It flickered from some unseen breeze and Ella began to wonder how much longer the stub of wax would last. She did not relish the thought of it being consumed. What would keep the rats at bay once there was not even the smallest bit of light to keep them scurrying from the shadows in which they currently hid?

With a hastily voiced *amen,* she gave up on her pleas to a higher being that He would save her from her fate. Her fate that Faramond would not see reason and release her. Her fate of finding herself wed to a man she did not love and living on the distant shores of Spain. She did not know how she would survive living on foreign land. She had had enough of a hard time adjusting to living in medieval England. How would she ever endure being gone from the few people she had become close to in her travels? More important than anything else… Her fate of losing Killian.

Killian… his name rushed across her soul causing her to gasp out, misery leaked from her eyes with the thought of never seeing him again. He had been right before her each and every time her feet had made their way to Berwyck. She had wasted so much precious time and now she would never have the chance to tell him of her feelings. She had been such a fool!

She pulled out the silver ring she had kept hidden in her gown to examine it closely. 'Twas a simple band with no further engravings, and she pondered who it might have belonged to that he would carry such a ring with him all these years. That he would give this same ring to her must mean there was no other woman in his life that he cared about.

Ella made her way to her pallet and pulled the thin-bare blanket up around her shoulders. The fabric barely touched the surface of the cold surrounding her heart. Henry… Simon… Killian… three men had come into her life. All three had served some purpose, but she had not given a flicker of attention to the one who mattered the most. She had thought only of returning to a man who did not even know her in his time. She had bent over backwards to keep herself in this time to be reunited with Henry when she should have concentrated on Killian. She had all but ignored the twinkling spark in his eyes whenever they were in each other's company. Ugh! Her life was a shamble. Her spirits were finally broken leaving her no hope that she could rebuild that which she discounted as nothing but friendship.

Hushed voices reached her ears and she wondered who approached. Ella stood, rushing to the bars of her cell when she heard a thud. Before she could call out, a body rolled down the stairs to be followed by the flickering light of a torch.

"Who goes there?" she called out, before squinting from the brightness of the light.

"'Tis me, my lady." Isabel stepped closer to the cell while a guardsman held the torch to light the lock. Keys jangled while her friend tried first one then another key. Ella held her breath while Isabel's attempts to open her cell sounded loud enough to wake the entire keep.

Ella did not realize she had been holding her breath 'til the air left her lungs in a loud whoosh when the bars of her prison swung open, ensuring her release. "Thank God, Isabel. You came for me, but at what cost?"

"'Tis not of import, Lady Ella. We must needs get you from this place."

Ella peered at the guardsman who waited with them. "You!" she fumed while recognizing the guard who had carried her down the majority of the way to this dungeon. "Why are you helping me now? You certainly were not coming to my aid before."

Isabel stepped between the two of them. "This is Sir Peter."

Ella could not believe this man had the nerve to show himself before her. "As if I care for his name," she sneered knowing the part the man before her played in having her in a dungeon of all places.

The knight raised his chin. "I am helping you only because of this woman," he replied, pointing to Isabel who smiled warmly at him. "Do you wish my help or not?"

Ella took askance to Isabel. "Can we trust him?"

Her friend nodded. "With our lives."

Ella was still wary. "What is the plan then? I cannot foresee me just walking out the front gates unnoticed."

Isabel handed her a bundle, while Sir Peter turned his back

to the women. "You are going to do just that, my lady. Put these on, and quickly," Isabel urged. "We do not have a lot of time before the guards change places."

Ella began pulling clothing from the bag Isabel thrust upon her. She smiled at the duplicity of the scheme as Isabel helped bind her breasts in linen. Ella took Killian's ring and tucked it inside the cloth before she quickly changed into hose, tunic, and boots. Isabel took a leather strap from her own hair and passed it to Ella who tied her hair up and covered it with a cap. When Isabel handed her a small container filled with a muddy concoction, she thought of the stories told of when Lady Amiria at Berwyck hid herself in a similar fashion, putting dirt upon her face to help hide her feminine features.

Ella worked quickly, applying the mixture to her face while trying not to gag from the stench of it. She decided to also smear some on her clothing. No one in their right mind would pay her the least bit of attention with the stench now emitting from her body. She looked for approval from her friend, who nodded her acceptance that Ella appeared as a small man. Isabel began collecting Ella's discarded clothing by shoving them into the bag and handing the bundle to her.

"We must needs make haste, ladies," the knight whispered into the darkness.

Ella took a deep breath. "I am ready." They began to pass by the unconscious guard upon the floor. "What of him? How did you manage to disarm the knight? Will he not know 'twas you who was his downfall?"

Sir Peter gave the man a nudge with the toe of his boot. "He shall sleep off what he unknowingly drank. If he is wise, he will say nothing for 'twill appear he was remiss in his duties by falling asleep, allowing your escape. Lord Faramond will not be pleased with him."

Ella had a sudden sense of foreboding awaiting the guard's fate. "I do not want him hurt because of me."

Peter nodded. "I shall see that no harm befalls him, my lady."

They began the climb up the narrow stairway, the flickering torches lighting the way to freedom. When they were almost at last at the top, Isabel halted their progress.

"My lady, this is where I must leave you. Do not rush when you are above ground but make haste once you are past the village. Hopefully you remember your way to Meaux Abby, and this is where Killian awaits you."

Ella turned to hug her friend. "I shall never forget what you have done this day for me, Isabel."

"Go, my lady, and God speed."

Ella watched as Isabel and Peter quickly disappeared topside. She smiled, wondering what their story was and mayhap one day she would still have the opportunity to ask.

With a deep breath, she took her first steps from her forced captivity. She passed unnoticed by the servants who were busy in the great hall, nor did anyone else pay attention to her while they went about their daily chores. She had a moment of panic when she passed through the kitchens and the Cook came at her with a raised pan in his meaty fist. He bellowed at the *man* who dared come into his domain reeking like he had spent the night in the stable yard.

Ella clutched her bundle containing her other clothing to her breast as she fled through the bailey and out the front gate, thankful there was no further hindrance with a guard halting her progress. 'Twas almost too easy, but she would ponder her good fortune once she was free of the place.

She made it to the forest edge where she took one last look at the keep, resting at its place near the River Hull. She wiped at a tear, knowing her son was beyond her reach. With a heavy heart, Ella made her way into the trees and began to run. She had no desire to be captured again.

CHAPTER 21

Killian said a final *amen* to his prayers. He had been coming here each morn and eve in the hopes that God above would hear his heartfelt plea for Ella's safety and deliverance from the evil that had taken her.

He nodded to one of the monks as he left the abbey's chapel. His purse was lighter after bargaining with the head priest on the only solution Killian could come up with to ensure Ella's son would no longer pursue them. Not that he cared about the monies he willingly forfeited. He would gladly give all he owned in the world in order for the woman he loved to be here with him now.

The monk had insisted they be compensated for the loss that would come to them, not to mention the lie that would need to pass from his lips. Killian had emphasized that no harm would come to the abbey itself. They had finally come to agreement after the hefty donation on Killian's part. He would set fire to one of the outer buildings and Faramond would be told his mother died in the flames. Their plan had to work and once Ella was back in his arms, he planned to never let her go again.

He made his way outside, shielding his eyes from the blinding sunlight. She should have been here by now. Killian was unsure how much patience he had left before he would make his way back to Hull and take her by force if necessary. He felt he could take down the damn keep stone by stone if need be, yet he knew such an action would only get him either killed or in a cell next to his woman.

He began pacing the courtyard of the abbey grounds when a figure appeared on the outskirts of the forest. A man by the looks or, rather, a lad given his smaller stature. He was dirty and looked weary from his travels. Yet there was something familiar about his stance that had Killian staring at the *man* who quickly approached after throwing down whatever *he* had been holding in his arms. And then it dawned on him, causing him to smile as he ran to her.

"Killian…" she called out as she, too, began to run.

"Ella…" he bellowed, holding out his hands toward her.

She flung herself into his body as his arms wrapped around her holding her close before his lips sought hers. He felt the tears cascading down her cheeks while his fingers caressed her face. He deepened their kiss before common sense took hold of his senses. He reluctantly pulled his lips from hers and at last took in her appearance, not to mention the smell emitting from the tiny woman before him. She had found a convincing way of making sure no one would come near her.

He gave a light-hearted chuckle and pulled at his beard. "Methinks ye be in need of a bath, my lady. Ye are too reminiscent of another young lass of our acquaintance who took tae a similar disguise when the enemy was at hand."

"Get me away from here and at a safe distance from my son and I shall be more than happy to bathe in the closest stream available."

He took hold of her hand. "Ye are well and no one followed ye?"

"For the most part, but let us away lest my son is following too close for my comfort." Ella looked over her shoulder as though Faramond would appear behind her at any moment. "I have spent the last two days hiding from the patrols he has sent out searching for me. 'Twill only be a matter of time before he heads toward the abbey, although I have been attempting to lead them away in any other direction but here."

"Ye are a clever woman, Ella Fitzpatrick," Killian murmured, impressed with her ability to survive off the land. Taking her hand, he led her to where she had dropped her bundle. "What have ye here?"

"My dress and some coin Isabel parted with, although I know not what she thought about giving me such a small fortune," she answered while gathering her meager belongings. "I would have been hard pressed to explain the garb if I had been questioned."

"Let us be thankful ye were not," he said, before heading in the direction opposite to whence she came.

Killian began to quicken his pace. There was a sense of urgency to get Ella far away from the abbey and her son. They made their way to the outer building he planned to raze. Mystic was already saddled and waiting for them. He turned, placing his hand around Ella's waist and lifted her onto the pillion. Taking her satchel, he thrust it into one of the bags and secured the fastener.

"Wait here," he ordered, before reaching for a torch he had

left hidden in the brush. He knelt upon the ground with flint in hand and began to work on lighting the pile of kindling that would ensure their escape. Quickly the fire started and Killian went inside the building and began to set aflame various piles of hay he had placed there the day before. Going back outside, he circled the building setting fire to the roof before tossing the near spent torch inside the doorway.

Making his way back to Ella, he leapt into the saddle before looking once more at the near engulfed building. With his heel, he nudged Mystic's side, causing the horse to bolt forward in his eagerness to get away from the building that would soon burn down to the ground.

Killian wasted no time finding the dirt road and set his horse to galloping in a south-western direction. He knew the general location of Conisbrough Castle and where Henry de Rune resided. He was relying on Ella's knowledge of the area in order for him to get her to the time gate at the correct hour... that is if she still wished to be with the knight.

Miles quickly passed them by, and he was beginning to feel as though he could at last breathe with the knowledge that Ella was safe. They came upon no one, which was either a blessing or a warning to be wary. He felt her grip his tunic tighter as though she had read his mind and he reached for her arm pulling her closer against his back. He could feel her hesitation.

"I do not wish ye tae fall off, Ella," he said, pulling on the reins to slow the animal beneath them as he made his way into the forest. He would need to find them shelter for the night, not to mention have speech with the lady.

"And I have no desire to find myself falling to the ground to be trampled beneath the hooves of this beast," Ella explained. "But considering how I can barely stand the smell of my own clothing, I do not wish to have your freshly washed garments reeking the same if I get too close."

He muttered an oath. "Yer son shall pay for his treatment of ye."

Her hand came to gently rest upon his forearm. "Forget him. I know I already have," she murmured but Killian did not miss the hurt resonating in the sound of her voice.

They came upon a slow running river and Killian kept Mystic in the water to erase their trail in case they were followed. Traveling at least another mile, Killian spotted a small inlet where another stream joined the waterway. He turned Mystic in that direction, making the decision they had traveled far enough this day. He raised his head to the sky. Night would fall soon. He would let Ella bathe in privacy while he went about finding them something for their supper.

Jumping down, he took the reins and led his steed farther into the forest to keep from being seen. He came upon a mossy area and, although 'twould not be as comfortable as a bed found in an inn, he could at least offer this to Ella to sleep upon.

He lifted her from Mystic and she stumbled into him when her knees buckled beneath her. Mumbling an apology, she set to work to get her things while Killian fumbled in his saddlebag for a bar of soap. Silently, he gave it to her while she nodded her thanks before taking herself from his sight.

He went about setting up camp before taking himself off into the woods to see what he could find to break their fast. He made sure he went in the opposite direction to that his lady had gone, certain he would have no self-control if he came upon her while she bathed.

Drawn to the billowing smoke seen when he came to a small rise, Faramond gave a might curse before making his way in the general direction of a well-known abbey. The smell of burning wood filled his nostrils when they neared. A monk came from a nearby chapel and a bellow of rage burst from Faramond's lips when the monk told him his mother had taken refuge inside what little remained of the dwelling.

Faramond fell to his knees in anguish... not from the news that mayhap his mother had taken her own life to be rid of her fate, but from the knowledge that all his scheming and planning to restore his title and good name were for naught. Tears came unbidden from his eyes. All was lost... he would never be the same. What would become of him now?

CHAPTER 22

The silence was deafening. Only the crackling fire penetrated the air around them as they finished their meal. Ella had been thankful earlier for the time alone to clean herself and her skin no longer felt like it was crawling with unseen bugs after her time in Hull's dungeon. The cold river had done wonders to revive her spirits. Now, here she sat contemplating the man before her. He was hard to read.

"Ella—"

"Killian—"

They spoke at the same time, as though they were both aware of what must be spoken between them. She set down her tin plate and watched as Killian did the same before he brushed at his beard with his fingers. Their eyes met across the dancing flames of the fire, causing Ella's breath to leap into her throat. She could guess what the man before her was thinking from the fleeting emotions that swept across his features. With her heart hammering inside her chest, she rose and came to sit next to the Scotsman who had saved her life in more ways than he knew.

"I cannot begin to thank you for all you have done for me of late," she began before taking his hand. His callused thumb began moving across her skin causing tiny goose bumps to race up her arm.

"Ye know I could do no less," he murmured. "'Twere a fair amount of time since I have had the opportunity tae save a fair damsel in distress." He chuckled in merriment at his own jest.

"'Tis far more than saving me from the fate awaiting me at Hull. You have been so patient with me in my attempts to come to terms with my life."

"Ye are safe now and 'tis all that matters."

"My safety is only a part of the issue here, Killian. I have been terribly confused of late."

"There is only one question that is of import, Ella." His mouth then opened and closed several times. He was apparently trying to find the right words while his eyes flickered with uncertainty. He reached over for a flagon she knew held some form of drink and took a long pull before he offered her a sip.

She put the flask to her lips hoping the alcohol would also help calm her nerves. "Go on," she murmured before handing him back the container. "I will answer any questions you may have."

"Are we close tae where you crossed time tae be with de Rune?" he asked, his tone gruff and strained.

"Aye," she said with remorse that she no longer wished to see Henry. "'Tis strange how I have known when I needed to be in certain places at particular times. Must be the Time Fairies having their way with me." She laughed, trying to make light of the heavy conversation she knew was coming.

"Do ye really wish for me tae take ye tae him, then?" he blurted out, his angry words echoing off into the woods.

Ella feared the reaction her decision might bring. Her answer would change not only everything she had been living for up to this point in her second chance at finding love, but also her relationship with Killian. Her hand rose up to his cheek while she caressed the softness of his whiskers with her fingertips. "That all depends on you," she finally answered, before dropping her hand, tilting her head to one side, studying the expression on his face.

"'Tis not for me tae decide. I have already told ye I will take ye wherever ye wish tae go. However, I canna read yer mind about who ye wish tae be with," he grumbled, turning his head towards the fire and away from her assessment of him.

"What if I told you the only place I want to *be* is with you. I now wish only to have a place inside your heart?"

"Do not jest with me, woman. I already feel I have been tae hell and back wondering how tae get ye out of that damned dungeon so I can claim ye as my own. I do not know how I would survive if I lost ye again, whether that be tae yer son or Time itself."

Reaching over, she gently turned his head toward her. "I am not jesting with you, Killian. 'Tis my heartfelt desire to always be with you."

She heard the air leave his lungs as if he had been holding his breath. "And what of de Rune?" he asked, with a raised brow. "I cannae readily dismiss how ye have cared for him all these years, but does he still own a piece of yer heart?"

Ella stood and began pacing before she turned to face him again. "I will not lie to you and say my feelings for Henry are all in the past. I am grateful to him. Falling through Time not once but twice has led me to you. If I had not followed this path, where would I be?"

"'Tis hard tae say. Time is fickle... or so I have heard from others who have crossed such an unbelievable barrier and come tae Berwyck's gates."

Ella nodded her head in agreement. "I may not have known at the time during my years of wandering, but, in truth, the person who I fell through Time for was not Henry. That man is the one I see sitting before me now."

"Ye can still be with him on the morrow if 'tis yer wish. Ye can change yer fate by simply telling me when we reach the place in the road near Conisbrough Castle and the Time gate."

"Aye... I suppose you have that aright if that was still my desire. 'Tis not even a day's ride from where we are now."

A groan left him while he stood before he began cleaning up what remained of their meal. "'Tis settled then. I will take ye there on the morrow and wish ye well."

"You daft man," she yelled out. "Have you not heard a word I have said about wanting to be with you?"

"But de Rune—"

"To hell with Henry! 'Tis you that I love, you stubborn oaf!"

Killian moved so quickly, Ella barely had time to react when he reached for her. As he pulled her close to his body, she could feel every inch of him, and her breath quickened with the realization he was aroused.

"Ye love me?" he asked before brushing her hair from her face.

"Aye, I love you," she shouted while giving him a push. He budged nary an inch and stood firmly in place. "Do you think if I scream it loud enough, my words might penetrate your thick Scottish brain?"

"Ye be a fiery woman, Ella Fitzpatrick," he murmured. His arms tightened around her.

"Aye and you better never forget it, Killian of Clan MacLaren."

"Ye can remind me again if I ever do," he replied, the low timbre of his voice causing her body to tremble.

"I never want to be parted from you again, but what of you? Have I made a mistake thinking you held some affection for me?"

"Nay, ye made no mistake. I love ye and desire tae be with ye, Ella, and no one else. For all of my days and even into the next world."

"Then kiss me, you fool, and stop arguing with me about Hen—"

His lips fell upon hers, hot and demanding as though he had been starving for her and no one else. 'Twas if he were taking possession of her and she tightened her arms around him.

Ella lost what little senses she had left when his tongue plunged inside her mouth. The taste of mead mingled on their breaths. Her knees buckled and before she knew what was happening, Killian lifted her up and carried her to a pallet he had made up for her.

He laid her down gently and she could sense the soft moss beneath her. Hovering above her, Killian seemed to be wavering with indecision.

"Killian?"

He came to lie down next to her yet held back from touching her. Leaning upon his elbow, he stared upon her. "Tell me tae leave ye now and I will, if I must. Otherwise, from this point forward I shall consider ye are mine and will fight tae the end of my days tae keep ye forever by my side."

She forced air into her lungs for clearly she had forgotten to breathe having him so close to her now. Her heart soared knowing Killian loved her. Reaching out, she placed her hand upon his arm and felt it tremble beneath her touch.

"My brave and fierce warrior..." she whispered, her arm snaking around his neck. "Please do not make we wait any longer to feel you completely next to me. Make me yours and love me, Killian." She gently urged his head forward.

"I already do, my lovely Ella."

Their kiss once more gave way to the burning passion they had been holding back for all this time. Clothes were discarded in a wild rush 'til their naked flesh melded together as limbs entwined around each other. Where Ella began, Killian ended and she cared not when his fevered apology cracked from his lips that he could wait no longer.

Ella cried out Killian's name when he entered her and she quickly followed his lead. She had waited a lifetime to unite with this man and at long last they were finally complete. Two halves were now whole. 'Twas as if the heavens smiled down upon their coupling for they were two reunited souls joined as one.

Ella's world shattered into a million fragments when she found her release. She clung to Killian as his moan of pleasure mingled with her own. Tears of joy streaked down Ella's cheeks when they floated back down from the rapture they found in each other's arms.

They touched. They laughed. They whispered words of love and held nothing back when they made love again as they explored one another this time at their leisure. Somewhere before dawn they finally slept, still tangled in each other's embrace. The heavens smiled. Love had found them.

CHAPTER 23

Killian awoke, startled by something that was amiss. He rubbed his eyes pondering what could possibly be wrong in his world when he and Ella at last came to a final accord and declared their love. Opening his eyes, he saw the day was wasting away if the height of the morning sun in a cloudless sky was any indication of the time.

'Twas then he heard the desperate sound of his lady's moan of despair. He pulled her closer into his embrace. Concern etched its way across his brow while he attempted to make out her incoherent words. Her body trembled and Killian frowned. What nightmare was she possibly re-living?

"My son," she moaned, then shrieked, "Faramond, no!"

Ella struggled within his arms and he released her, afraid he might do her more harm if he continued his attempts to hold her close to his side. She bolted upright while throwing her head back, tears streaming down her face.

She gasped before her gaze darted around their campsite and

then leveled upon him. "Killian..." her voice trailed off as though she still was gripped in the dreams that had tormented her while she slept.

"Good morn, my love," he said, bringing her back down to lay her head upon his chest. He kissed the top of her head and grabbed at the blanket to cover her while she continued to shiver in his arms.

"Is it? Still morning that is?" she asked while she clung to him.

"Aye. We should break camp and get started tae Berwyck."

"Berwyck?"

"I have no other place tae call home. I assumed ye would wish tae make a home with me there. Was I mistaken?" He held his breath while awaiting her answer.

"Of course… Berwyck, and nay, you were not mistaken." She tore herself from his arms as though she was angry with him and picked up her discarded clothes scattered upon the ground from the night before.

He stood and donned his own garments while Ella quickly dressed. He gazed upon her for several minutes when she began cleaning up their camp. 'Twas obvious she was troubled, and he would not start their life together by ignoring her and clearly upset with whatever she had dreamed.

Killian went to her. "Ella, stop," he said taking her hand and going to sit on a log near the dying embers of their fire. "What is troubling ye? Do ye regret last night?"

"What?" she gasped, her hand going to her throat as if his words caused her further torment. "Nay, of course I have no regrets."

He nodded. "Then what were ye dreaming about that caused ye so much pain?"

She looked at him with worried eyes. "'Tis nothing."

"Ye are not fooling me by saying *'tis nothing*. I can see for myself ye are not yerself. Tell me," he urged before taking her hand and bringing it to his lips.

Her breath left her in a sudden rush. "'Twas just a nightmare…"

"… that has left ye troubled that yer dream may come true," he surmised, and her eyes widened at his words. So that was the problem.

"How did you know?"

"'Tis not hard tae assume, given ye are still shaking from yer visions. What were they?"

"'Twas my son."

"Yer son would give anyone nightmares considering what he has done tae his own mother," Killian muttered, "but go on."

"I dreamt whomever the man was that Faramond made the arrangement with that I marry, well… he took offense when I was not at Hull." Her chest heaved while taking another breath.

"I suppose if I were in the man's place, I could understand his plight."

"But I saw my son's head on a pike outside the gates of the keep," she cried out before she threw herself into his lap. Her arms wound their way around his neck and he felt her tears again. He could stand anything, but not her tears.

"'Twas just a dream," he replied, in a small attempt at offering her comfort.

"I am n-not s-so c-certain," she stammered before hugging him tighter. She took several deep breaths as though to compose herself. "I cannot easily dismiss such a vision as just a dream that will not come true upon the morrow."

"We knew Faramond was beyond thinking rationally, Ella,

elsewise he wouldnae have arranged a marriage for ye that would only serve his own purpose and that of the king."

"Aye, I know what you are saying is true, but he is still my son."

"A son should have more respect for the woman who gave him the very air he breathes and life," he grumbled. At some point in the night, Ella had told him of the events that shaped Faramond's anger, but the boy had chosen to hold on to his hate and turn it on his own mother. Killian had no respect for the man Ella's son had become.

"Yet he is still my flesh and blood, and the only child I will ever have. What can I do to save him from such a fate if my dreams are a premonition of what is to come? If only..." she hiccupped as she gulped in air and he barely heard her whispered words when she continued, "...I could turn back the hands of time."

Killian clutched Ella in a fierce embrace even while his chest tightened and his stomach roiled. Everything fell into place as though Heaven itself whispered to him the answer to Ella's dilemma. Or mayhap 'twas those same Time Fairies playing their games on him as they had done to Ella. He knew what he must do for the woman he loved.

He kissed her 'til he felt her response. "Let us away before we miss our opportunity," he said taking her hand as she rose from his lap.

"What opportunity?" she asked.

"Tae right a wrong," he murmured, but at her quizzical look, he shrugged his shoulders in a firm resolve to stand by the decision he had yet to voice to the woman who meant all to him. He had the feeling Ella was going to be spitting mad at him. She would hate him for the plan he had only just formed in his head but hopefully would one day forgive him.

Luck was on his side for she did not question him further. They broke camp quickly for there was not much to pack and before long they were once more in the saddle, with Ella riding behind him. They had not ridden far before Ella voiced her concern that Killian knew was coming.

She tugged upon his tunic and he glanced behind him but continued on. "I may not be much of a horsewoman, my love, but I do have a sense of direction. You are going the wrong way to Berwyck."

"Aye, I am well aware which direction is home."

"Then where are we going?"

"Ye know where," he said as if she should be reading his thoughts.

"But this is the way to Conisbrough!" she exclaimed, giving his tunic a mighty yank.

"Aye and ye are going tae change yer son's fate and maybe yer own," he answered.

"You cannot possibly be suggesting that I fall through Time again!"

"Ye are a smart woman, Ella. Of course, I am suggesting ye fall through Time again."

"It cannot be done just as I am too late for the meeting with Henry."

"I have given thought to that, my lady. If this is the right thing – and I feel in my heart that 'tis, then Time shall take ye back to the point at which ye met Henry."

"People's lives could change… everything between *us* could change."

"Ye will remember *us*, Ella, just as surely as I will remember *ye*."

"How can you be so sure?" Her words lowered to barely a whisper. "How can you do this to us?"

"Ye ask too many questions, Ella," he answered gruffly not voicing the overwhelming uncertainty warring inside his head.

They fell into silence as they continued through the forest 'til the sudden urge to halt Mystic overcame him. A sob was torn from his lady's lips.

"For the love of God, Killian, get me the hell away from here!"

If there was any doubt left that they had reached the place where Ella had fallen through Time, her heartfelt cry of distress confirmed they had arrived. Jumping down from the saddle, he pulled Ella down while she began to fight him.

"Damn you, Killian!"

"Easy now, woman," he yelped as a fist near hit his eye.

"Easy now?" she screamed. "You Scottish arse! You expect me to take it easy when you wish me to go and live hell on earth for a second time? Nay! 'Twill be more like a third or fourth lifetime I must live in order for me to find you again. You ask too much of me, Killian!"

"Ye can do it, Ella," he grunted out when her well-aimed fist landed in his belly. He trapped her swinging arms when he pulled her to him before they did more damage.

"You know not what you are asking of me," she cried out yet again while she clung to him.

He held her away from him even though it almost cost him his heart to see the anguish in her eyes. He held up a finger then gave her a quick kiss. "One—Stay with de Rune 'til 'tis time for ye tae slip through—"

"How can you so easily talk of me going to another man?"

"I cannae stand the thought of another man being with ye or loving ye," he growled out with furrowed brows before he continued where he had left off. "Find the second time gate and go tae the inn so ye and Simon meet. Save yer son by ensuring yer husband does not send him away."

Her hands reached up to clasp her head as though pained. "You know how families send their sons to squire with other lords. Faramond will be no different. Simon will never agree."

"Then ensure he goes tae some other lord who ye trust. Surely ye will know of someone who will properly train yer son and not abuse him."

"Do you forget I do not *know* anyone other than Simon from thirty years ago? I am completely alone in a foreign time and place, Killian," she yelled out. "Just who the hell do you think I would entrust with my son?

"Ye will think of someone."

She let out a loud groan. "You are not helping me solve my dilemma! This is *not* like I am going to take a leisurely stroll by the beach," Ella fumed.

Raising a second finger, he kissed her again. "Two—never tell Faramond of yer origins."

Ella shook her head in denial. "That fact alone will change me from wandering England for all those years. 'Tis the reason I met Katherine. 'Tis why I made my way to Berwyck. How am I to explain my absence from Hull?"

"Ye will figure something out," Killian replied, before he lifted another finger and kissed her even longer this time. "Three—As ye said, save Katherine de Deveraux from the waters of the Coquet River and bring her tae Berwyck. Travel tae the castle from time tae time and treat me as you have done before we made this journey together. Do not forget tae have speech with Jenna Sinclair when she, too, falls through Time and ends up at Berwyck."

Ella stomped her foot. "Just how the hell am I supposed to know exactly *when* I am to be doing all this for a second time, you idiot?" she yelled at him again before punching him in the chest. "'Tis not like I have a modern-day calendar I can consult!"

Since he had no notion what this *calendar* thing was she spoke of, he took her wrist, before unclenching her fingers and bringing them to his lips. "Ye said ye went on a pilgrimage, did ye not? Pray. God will answer by telling ye in yer heart where ye need tae be and when."

"You seem so sure of all this, and yet why do I feel like you are trying to get rid of me?"

He puffed out his chest and folded his arms. "Get rid of ye? Are ye daft, woman? I am trying tae help ye so ye can save yer son." He led her over to a small babbling brook.

Kneeling down, Ella cupped her hands to splash water over her face 'til her head looked up and she gazed upon the area. "Good Lord! Do you know this is the same area where I saw my younger self when I fell through Time the second go around?"

"Ella..." She quickly stood and threw herself into his arms leaving Killian doubting he was doing what he knew in his heart was right.

"I cannot do this, Killian. Please... Let us ride to Berwyck and forget this whole business of me slipping through Time again," Ella pleaded with him. Her words almost broke his heart.

"We cannae, my love. Ye would always regret not trying tae save yer son, and I couldnae live with myself knowing I did not give ye the opportunity tae right a wrong. I know 'twill work if ye but try." He took her by the elbow and led her to a small rise on the edge of the forest, the road but a short distance away. The sound of a horse galloping in the distance caused him to pull Ella into his arms.

"Killian... please, I beg of you... do not do this to us," she implored while taking hold of the edges of his tunic.

He leaned down and kissed her with all the love he had for her in his heart. The sound of the horse drew closer, oddly distorted as if it had traveled through a barrier. "Remember all I have said and what ye must do. 'Tis of grave import, especially for the well-being of yer son and the Lady Katherine."

"I love you, Killian," she whispered.

"And I love ye, Ella. Throughout all time will I love only ye."

She began fumbling in her gown 'til she held out the ring he had given her. "I need to return this to you," she said while her hands began to shake.

He closed her fingers, the ring secure in the palm of her hand. "Ye must keep it so ye remember me always," he said before kissing her forehead.

"I am scared. Kiss me again so I know you will remember me," she said as though she, too, had come to terms with what she must do.

He gave in to her demand and his heart lurched when he tore his lips from hers. "I could never forget ye, Ella. I shall be jealous of every starlit night ye gaze upon, the sun as it beams down upon ye on a cloudless day, and even the rain that falls tae yer face tae mingle with yer tears. Forget ye..." he murmured while stroking her cheek. "'Twould be like forgetting tae breathe, my love."

"What will I do without you?"

Before he could answer, their heads turned. The sound of the horse was almost upon them, but they saw nothing. Killian quickly kissed Ella as though for the last time then took her by the hand, edging her closer through the trees. His eyes widened when he witnessed a distortion upon the road and saw for himself the Time gate Ella must pass through.

"Remember me, Ella, and do not forget that love will find ye," he whispered before placing a quick kiss upon her forehead.

"Killian... I love y—"

"Forgive me, my dearest love," he said cutting off her words even as he gave her a mighty shove.

"Killian! N-n-n-no!"

He watched fear etch itself across her visage when she stumbled towards the Time gate. He saw her hovering in the air before Time swallowed her up and the gate vanished. The sounds of the horse vanished. He gulped at the implications of what this may have cost him.

Despair filled his very soul. *My God, what have I just done?* He made his way to the brook before he fell to the ground to splash water on his face. But Killian was unprepared when he saw his hands begin to vanish before his very eyes.

"By St. Michael's Wings!" he cried out.

One moment he was in the forest hating what he had done to Ella and the next he was floating in a cloud of nothingness as though Time was to play a cruel twist of fate on him just as he had done to Ella. He yelled out her name, praying he would remember her.

PART II
THE THIRD TIME'S THE CHARM

CHAPTER 24

Conisbrough Castle
The Year of Our Lord's Grace, 1182
A brief moment in Time later…

Ella slowly awoke and took in her surroundings. Seeing where she was, she closed her eyes and opened them again, hoping the scene before her would be different. But nay, nothing had changed as she came to the realization that he had pushed her. *Pushed her! Damn that stupid Scotsman to hell.*

Her gaze fell to the man before her while he changed a cool cloth upon her forehead. Henry… those green eyes were just as she remembered them, along with the concern etched upon his features. His blond hair had once been so flattering upon him but now she favored a brown-reddish hue. She pushed Killian's image from her mind, as hard as that was. She felt as though she was betraying what they felt for one another but in truth, had they even met yet in this version of Time? She could not help but wonder if she was on his mind. If she went looking for him, would he remember her?

She had a matter of grave import to accomplished, she remembered, as she came out of her musings to stare at the man before her... lord of his castle but struggling financially to keep his estate. Funny how Henry was now staring upon her as though they had never crossed paths at Warkworth. Time had an odd way of playing with people. Ella was not certain she could go through this all over again and yet what choice did she have? How strong did God, and Killian for that matter, think she truly was?

"You were lucky you were not trampled to death, my lady," Henry said, sitting back in the chair near her bedside. "What were you doing traipsing in the forest alone?"

"I was lost," she answered in a hoarse whisper. Her throat was dry. "Water?"

"Wine," he said holding out a nearby chalice for her to take as she rose upon the bed holding the coverlet in front of her.

"How long have I been here?"

"Long enough," he replied giving her no answer at all. "I feared you might not awake after your fall."

She felt her head. Just a bruise, so she was lucky for a second time in her life. 'Twas then she realized something was missing. Pulling back the coverlet, she gasped in surprise. "Where the hell are my clothes?"

He gave her a roguish grin as though he could hear her thoughts while she believed the worst of him. "Have no fear, my lady. I had one of my servants, a woman, see to the removal of your garments so we could ensure you had no broken bones after your accident."

A moment of panic consumed her before her eyes landed on

Killian's ring shining in the candlelight on a table by the bed. A heavy sigh of relief escaped her before she returned her attention to the man before her. Ella clutched the coverlet, bringing the fabric up to her chin. "And you could not do this with my clothes *on*, my lord?"

"I can see you are distraught from your ordeal," he murmured not offering an apology, before standing and going to the hearth to bank the fire.

"You, sir, have no idea of how distraught I truly am," she complained.

"Mayhap introductions are in order. I am Lord Henry de Rune of Conisbrough Castle. Who… are you?"

"You do not remember me?" she asked, curious if he had even the slightest recollection of meeting her at Warkworth.

He cocked his head as though pondering the matter. "I am certain I would recall you if we had met before, especially considering you were almost trampled by my horse. Do you not remember your name?"

"I remember who I am," she whispered while she did everything in her power to think on this as their first meeting. "I am Ella."

"Ella of…" he watched her carefully, as though trying to figure her out.

"Just Ella," she answered, thinking her last name might not be in her best interest. She still had to stay with this man at least for a while. She could not see herself falling in love with him all over again, but she knew for certain she must act the way she had before. She remembered how terrified she had been when she had been thrown back in time. How he had scoffed at her words when she told him she was not of his world.

"I see… Mistress Ella."

She peered at him. Was she mistaken, or was that a flicker of disappointment in his tone? Distaste? She was not certain but had no opportunity to ponder it further when he continued.

"I shall leave you to rest and will have a servant fetch you something to eat. Mayhap on the morrow, if you feel up to it, I can show you my estate," he gave her a gentle, if not welcoming, smile.

She gave a short nod and his smile widened in response. "That would be lovely, Lord de Rune."

"Call me Henry," he answered, with a wink, before taking his leave.

Ella's breath left her in a sudden rush. She swore then and there when she got her hands on Killian, she was going to strangle that man to within an inch of his sorry life!

CHAPTER 25

Ella stood in Henry's solar. She had to admit the past two months had easily slipped away. Still, it had been a challenge as she relived everything she had done with the man before her. She had been wooed... period. She now remembered why she had fallen in love with this man the first time around. She now understood why she had held that love close to her heart for nigh unto thirty years when she had been thrown through the second Time gate. Understood why she had wished to return to him.

Henry had done everything right to convince Ella that he loved her. Except for one thing, her heart would be dangerously close to forgetting the future, just as she had done last time. She only needed to proclaim she would stay here with him and she could dismiss all the rest... or could she? For still the same problem existed, however, and in that aspect, nothing had changed... except for Ella.

As she listened to his words, her stomach flipped and made her nauseous. What was wrong with her? 'Twas not like she was not prepared for this conversation.

"Please listen to reason, my dearest love," Henry tried again with his plea.

Ella gave a heavy sigh. She knew what was coming. Today was as good a day as any to slip through Time again. "I am not your dearest love, Henry."

"Why, of course you are, my sweet," he beamed.

He was giving her *the look*, as if those green smoldering eyes of his could persuade her into changing her mind. She was unsure why she never saw this side of Henry before now. Perchance her situation with him before was all based on her desperate need to be loved and he had been the one to come to her rescue. Although she had been acting to the best of her ability as if she cared so their situation together could be played out, she was not in love with him as she had been some thirty years ago.

Her stomach lurched again. "If I were, you would not be planning to marry someone young enough to be your daughter." The words tumbling from her mouth called to mind a middle-aged man having a mid-life crisis as in modern days.

His face changed with her words. Indifference. Contempt. And above all boredom, as though her words and feelings held no worth. He was too used to getting his way and she could clearly see she had overstepped the boundaries set in place between them. His raised brows told her much of what was going to spill from his mouth next. Her thoughts were right on target when he spoke.

"Our marriage will ensure I remain in favor with the King,

along with her monies to replenish my estate." His gaze went to the parchment before him as he took up the quill, and Ella assumed he signed his name to the marriage document.

"And what of love, Henry?" *Where did those words come from?* she mused.

"*Love*? What does love have to do with any of this?" he scoffed, before folding up the parchment.

"It has everything to do with the way we live our lives, Henry. Life without love is meaningless. Do you not wish to be happy with the woman you shall wed?"

A strange sound escaped his lips before he composed himself again. "You own my heart. She will bear my heir and nothing more." He took wax and held it over the candle, then let it drip over the document. Taking off his signet ring, he stamped the melted wax and sealed his fate… and hers.

"I wish you to be happy, Henry," she whispered and, in her heart, she meant it. Everyone deserved to be loved despite the current custom of arranged marriages for nothing more than convenience and wealth.

"I shall be very happy," he mused aloud giving her a bright smile. "I shall ensure your place in my household and have my lady wife make you one of her attendants. I shall visit your chambers once she is with child. Nothing shall change between you and me."

Her eyes widened at his words, even while a small piece of her heart cracked wide open. *Oh my God!* She was going to throw up. *That* bit of conversation never happened before but, despite this fact, his words still crushed her spirits.

"How convenient for you," Ella managed to croak out. Tears, unbidden, leaked from her eyes to rush down her cheeks. The urge to flee from the keep overwhelmed her as though the Time Fairies were telling her she must hurry through their gate.

"Come now. Why do you cry?" he asked, coming to stand before her. He took her hands and, despite his words, an unwelcome shiver of delight passed through her body as a grim reminder of what she once felt for this man.

"How can you ask me such a question?"

"I have been nothing but upfront with you. I told you this marriage had been arranged. We can still be together."

"With me stashed away as your mistress?"

He shrugged. "Aye, although you have not shared my bed as yet, 'tis the best I can offer you. Since you have no wealth of your own to bring to our union if we were able to wed, how else do you expect me to save my lands?" He lowered his head while continuing to caress her fingers.

She snatched her hands away before he could place a kiss upon her skin. "I will be no man's mistress and we shall never be together, Henry."

Turning from him, she fled the room even while she heard him bellowing out her name. She ran down the turret steps, through the hall, and out of the keep. She continued to hear him calling for her to return even while she made her way through the bailey and out the barbican gate.

Angry tears for wasted time, rushed down her face as she made her way toward the forest. But it was the sound of horses and wagon wheels that made her hesitate. Turning back to gaze up at the castle, she saw Henry's future wife as she made her way down the road. Her covered wagon was a clear indication of her station in life as she traveled with a full complement of retainers, along with her standard flying in the afternoon breeze.

Ella turned her back on the scene and ran into the forest.

Falling to her knees, she gasped for breath before her stomach heaved and she lost what little food she had eaten that morn. Wiping her mouth, she rose, her feet practically flying down a path now looking strangely familiar. With her last fleeting thoughts of Henry, she stumbled into the glowing ring on the trail and once more slipped through time...

CHAPTER 26

Berwyck Castle
The Year of Our Lord's Grace, 1153

Killian of Clan MacLaren swung his blade and watched in satisfaction when the sword of the knight before him was knocked from the man's hands. The knight stepped back in surrender and yielded their match, much to the crowd's delight. 'Twas nothing like winning a tourney event, lest it was to have a fair-looking woman beneath him.

He marched his way over to the covered platform where his Laird and the Lady of Berwyck clapped their hands. Laird Douglas's sister Lady Freya stood as she, too, clapped her enthusiasm that he had won the match. He bowed before them, then winked at one of Lady Catherine's lady attendants who stood behind her.

Laird Douglas raised his chalice in a salute. "Well done, Killian. I would expect nothing less from one of my clansmen."

Killian nodded. "If ye are pleased, my laird, then so am I. I am yer humble servant."

Douglas laughed. "Ye? Humble? I have known ye all my life and ye were never one tae boast about being humble. I think arrogant is a better description," he quipped while leaning on the arm of his chair.

"Ye injure my pride, my laird, tae think such of me," Killian replied with a devilish smile, causing the women behind Lady Catherine to giggle.

Lady Catherine looked behind her and the laughter quickly subsided. He gulped, not wishing to offend a woman he held in the utmost respect. Laird Douglas had wed his lady last year at Henry, the Duke of Normandy's, command. Although an Englishwoman, she had managed to fit in with the clan as though she had been born here. Killian was not sure if he believed in love at first sight but such had been the case in the meeting between the pair. The tournament was a celebration for the villagers of Berwyck, both those who lived in the castle and those who tilled the fields.

Lady Catherine reached over and took her husband's hand and a look passed between them that was not hard to miss. "Stop teasing him, my laird, elsewise you shall never get a day's rest. Killian will no doubt challenge you so he may redeem his honor in your eyes. Knowing the two of you, as I already do, you shall be hacking away at each other 'til the moon is high in the sky."

Douglas took her fingers and raised them to his lips. "I cannae deprive ye of my charming company for so long, my lady."

"See that you do not," Catherine chided with a twinkle in her eyes. "You see, Killian, your honor is intact. Is this not so, Douglas?"

"Aye, ye have that aright, wife," Douglas proclaimed. "Come join us, Killian, and we will raise a cup to your victory upon the field."

"I would happily join ye, my laird, but I fear the stench of me after all the matches may cause the fair ladies in yer party tae faint. Mayhap ye would indulge me by allowing me tae clean up first?"

Douglas waved his hand with another chuckle. "Off ye go then but do not keep these ladies waiting long else ye may find they are already spoken for."

"Aye, my laird." Killian bowed. "Ladies..."

He left to the sound of their giggles but had not gone far before he heard his name being called. 'Twas the Lady Beatrice, who was one of Lady Catherine's attendants, and he could not be more pleased to see that she sought to follow him.

He took her hand and pulled her behind one of the many tents that had been erected between the tourney field and the castle. She willing went into his arms, wrapping her arms around his neck despite the chainmail between them. She smelled of wildflowers and he inhaled the scent from her hair 'til he felt her pushing on his tabard.

"Killian... you smell, dear," she murmured with a tinkling laugh that caused a part of him to stir to life.

He nuzzled her neck. "Ye asked permission tae leave?" he muttered as he moved to her ear.

"Aye." Beatrice's sigh of contentment was like the sweetest music to his ears.

"Good! I wouldnae wish ye tae get into trouble with yer lady."

"Killian when are you going to ask—"

He silenced her words when he placed his mouth to hers, plunging his tongue past her lips as though he was a man starving. In a way he was. How long had it been since he had a woman beneath him? Far too long, he supposed, but he knew what the lady would be asking next. When did he plan to ask for them to marry? Marry? There were far too many women in the world for him to settle for just one. At a score and seven he was not ready to settle down, at least not yet, and certainly not with Beatrice. She was a pleasant diversion but he had also seen she had become flirtatious since her arrival at Berwyck. He would not take such a woman as his wife. To bed, aye, but nary to wed.

A sharp pain on the top of his head caused Killian to break off the kiss and turn in anger to see who dared interrupt them. "What the bloody hell," he cursed and saw an older woman, heavy with child, holding a stick pointed at him. Mistress Shona, Berwyck's healer, was none too pleased with him at the moment. He tended to stay clear of her and her queer ways, always telling people what they did not want to hear.

"What do ye think ye be doing, young Killian," the woman chastised him before pointing to Lady Beatrice. "Ye best be on yer way, good woman. Killian is not for ye, so ye best not be setting yer sights on him. Now, shoo!"

He watched the woman he had been ready to have a tumble with scamper away. "What did ye do that for?" he moaned. "And what nonsense were ye preaching about her not being for me? 'Tis none of yer business who I bed."

"Stop acting like a spoiled bairn." She brandished her stick in front of him like she carried a mighty sword. "Or do ye wish me tae knock some more sense into that thick Scottish skull of yers?"

Killian crossed his arms over his chest. He was far too old to be reprimanded by this tiny woman who could see things that had yet to come to pass. He was careful to keep his distance from her whenever possible. 'Twas only when he had some injury during his training or fighting on the outskirts of the castle that he had need of her aid. Otherwise he had no notion to listen to whatever she would go sputtering on about.

"Well?" she asked, giving him a nudge with her stick since he had obviously not heard a word she said.

"What is it ye want from me, Mistress Shona?"

"At last, ye show me some respect. There may be hope for ye after all. Come with me," she urged while taking his arm before he even offered it to her.

They made their way toward the castle, crossing the bridge with the dry moat far below, and at last through the barbican gate to reach the inner bailey. When they reached her hut, she set down the stick she had used to smack him and also as an aid to help her walk, although Killian doubted she needed such a device. She was not *that* old. But mayhap the child she carried pained her. Should not the woman be in confinement and not traipsing about for everyone to ogle her in such a state?

"Come in, come in," she urged waving him inside while holding her lower back. "'Tis at last time and I can now tell ye many things ye will need tae know as ye go through yer life."

"And this cannae wait?"

Her brow rose while she studied him before she went to her fire, tsk, tsking as she went. "Ye youth are too full of yerself. Always in such a hurry ye are. Never take time tae listen tae what is good for ye."

"But Lady Beatrice is waiting for me. 'Tis not proper tae keep a lady waiting," he said with a wicked smile.

She slammed her mortar and pestle upon the table. "Ye would be wise tae stay away from her. She be trouble and will take ye down a road ye may not wish tae follow."

He laughed and snorted at the same time. "She is naught but a woman..."

"...who will be the ruin of ye and yer hopes for the future if ye continue this path!"

"For heaven's sake, what path? She is but a diversion. Someone tae satisfy my needs. I have no intention tae marry her."

"Well that is all good and said but if ye get her belly full with yer babe, ye will anger her father. She is not a woman ye should trifle with."

"Fine! I will leave her alone. There are others who are more than willing tae share my bed."

"Fool!"

"Fool? Why do you call me a fool and, in truth, why are we even having this conversation, woman?"

Shona shook a spoon at him. "Ye best remember yer tongue, Killian, lest ye find I put something in yer supper and ye cannae eat for a week."

His chest puffed out with pride. "Ye willnae dare."

"Talk tae me in that manner again and ye will find out!"

Killian shuffled his feet. "What is it ye see, Mistress Shona? I have the feeling I willnae like it."

She came over and took his arm and sat him in a chair. She pulled another one close to him. Taking his hand she began examining the lines before she closed her eyes. "There will be but one woman who shall belong tae ye. She comes from another place..."

"France?" he asked interrupting her.

"...in time," she finished while scowling at him. "She comes tae ye from afar, farther than ye could travel by foot or by sea. In fact, ye shall not meet her for several years."

"Years? Ye must needs be jesting with me, mistress. Am I tae remain celibate 'til I meet this mysterious woman?"

"Perchance."

"Ye cannae expect me tae wait a year for some lady I have yet tae meet, Shona," he growled out.

"Did I say a year?" she said with a small smile. "'Twill be far longer than a year's time I am afraid."

His breath left him. This conversation was getting out of hand and yet something inside his head was whispering for him to play close attention to what Berwyck's healer had to say.

"Five years?" he asked watching Shona shake her head. "Ten?" Again, she gave a negative shake of her head. "I shall be an old man by the time another ten years pass.

"'Tis more like a score and ten," she answered as she sat back in her chair. "But Time is a fickle mistress and such an outcome mayhap change. Ye shall have tae wait and see. She shall be worth the wait, Killian."

"How much wine have ye been drinking this day? Surely ye are but jesting with me. I may not wish tae wed today but I do wish tae have a wee bairn or two with a woman I take tae wife. I willnae wait almost a score and ten some years for a woman I can only then claim as my own. Why, I shall be lucky if I even live so long."

"Ye shall live, Killian. The lady will travel to Berwyck from time tae time but she must never learn that ye know of her. There are aspects of her life that she must complete before the two of ye can at last be together."

"And just how will I know this person is the woman ye are

saying is destined for me?" he growled out. "There are lots of people who venture to Berwyck."

"Ye shall know. Just remember… 'tis of import that ye heed my words about allowing this time tae pass between ye, else ye shall ruin more than yer own future."

"I hear them," he grumbled, yet there was a slight nagging inside his head when Shona spoke of this mysterious lady he would one day meet. But he ignored such a whispering, for his only wish was to get the hell out of the healer's hut and drown himself in wine. Mayhap if he got drunk some of this conversation might make sense.

"She will be worth waiting for, Killian," she repeated. "Ye but need tae trust me…"

He left the hut and went toward the stables to thoroughly dunk his head in the horse trough. He was not sure if the water cleared his head from the jumbled thoughts racing across his mind but at least his face was clean. *What did some middle-aged woman know anyway?* he mused.

Making his way to the garrison hall, he went to his room and changed into clean garments before heading back toward the tourney field. *Now… where had Lady Beatrice gone?* He went in search of the lady as though his talk with Mistress Shona had never occurred.

CHAPTER 27

The Oak Tree Tavern
The Year of Our Lord's Grace, 1153

Ella sat at a corner table, her back to the wall while she clutched the cup of ale in trembling hands. Hands that were no longer aged by time. Hands that were young again just like the rest of her body. If only they would stop shaking.

Gazing at her younger self in the reflection of the water had still been just as shocking as it had been the first time. She had rinsed her mouth out before picking up the hem of her dress and started walking in the direction of the tavern. She knew the way. She had been there before.

Luckily, she had sewn a few coins into the hem of her gown so she was not completely without monies on the off chance the time for meeting Simon was not yet. She doubted such would be the case, which was why her eyes continually went to the tavern door each time it opened. Still… she kept expecting to witness another version of herself creeping into the tavern but at least that had not happened. Apparently, Time was indeed a master manipulator and in this instance she was grateful she was not ripping open the fabric of Time. 'Twas one less thing to worry over!

Ella took a drink then put her head in her hands. She was not sure how much more she could take, even while she knew she was destined for living her life all over again. She briefly pondered how many times she would recite that mantra in her immediate future. *Shit!* Just the thought of existing almost another thirty years before laying eyes on Killian again just about broke her heart... Thirty years until she could kiss him again! That is if she did not kill him first.

A gust of wind blew through the room while the candles flickered on the walls when the door opened to admit a weary traveler. She would have recognized him anywhere. A person did not forget the father of ones child and her breath seemed trapped in her throat when the knight pulled back the hood of his cloak and made his way toward the barkeep. His black curly hair was just as unruly as she remembered, his shoulders just as broad. If she had not been so in love with Henry at the time of her encounter with Simon, she would have appreciated the handsome man who had come to love her. Tall, with light blue eyes, he appeared so much like their son that tears welled in her eyes. Ella realized she had cared for him after all.

He turned at the bar, leaning an elbow on the edge while he took a sip from his tankard. Their gazes met across the space between them, his eyes widening as he inspected her. He cocked his head to one side as though debating whether or not he should seek her out.

Ella knew this outcome, just as she knew others that would

happen between them, so she had no issue when Simon made his way across the room to stand before her table.

He held out his hand to the vacant bench. "May I?"

She knew she must not appear so eager. As far as Simon was concerned, they were strangers. "Sit?" she asked and at his nod, she casually took a sip from her cup before setting it down. She waved her hand about the room. "There are plenty of other places to take your ease. Choose another table."

"Ah... I see," he said, taking another drink while his eyes swept the other occupants of the tavern.

Ella folded her hands in her lap. "See what, good sir?"

"You are awaiting your husband, of course."

"I assure you, I am not married nor am I waiting for a husband to join me."

"A young woman with your fine looks unwed?" he questioned good-naturedly. "Why, I can hardly believe my good fortune."

Her lips twitched at the compliment. It had been so long since they had teased one another. "I see not how my marital status, or lack thereof, is any of your concern."

"Any man who would not take you to wife is a fool," he murmured before sliding across the bench to sit across from her.

"You do not even know me," she answered with a raised brow.

"Call it intuition. How many fools have let you slip through their grasp?"

"I have only encountered one of late who would fit such a description," she laughed, "present company not included."

Simon's chuckle was a familiar reminder of her previous time with this gentleman before her. He would, after all, be Faramond's father one day. "I suspect there may come a time when you may also call me a fool."

"Only time will tell, sir," Ella replied with a smirk.

"Mayhap we should introduce ourselves. I am Lord Simon of Hull and who is the enchantress before me that I cannot take my eyes from?"

"Ella," she replied, again giving no more information to Simon than she had to Henry.

Simon reached across the table for her hand and kissed her fingertips. "'Tis indeed a pleasure, *ma cherie*."

A shiver raced through her body, welcomed despite the love she felt for Killian. She shook her head knowing what was in store for her. She would not give any further thoughts to her Scotsman tonight. This moment belonged to Simon. She offered him a small smile. "My lord…"

He watched her carefully and finally realized he still held her fingers in his hand. He released them, and Ella swore she saw a hint of regret when he did so.

"Mistress Ella…" his words trailed off as though he was as confused as she had been when they had first met.

"Aye?"

"You may find this strange but I feel as though I know of you."

"I assure you, we have never met before this eve."

"The moment I espied you across the room, I felt compelled to make your acquaintance. Have you ever experienced the like?" His smile was wary yet she could see the joy on his face while small lines crinkled near his eyes.

"Not 'til I met you," she whispered.

He held his palm upwards on the table. A simple offering,

yet the implication was monumental at least in Ella's mind. She took his hand. Let their journey begin...

CHAPTER 28

Hull Castle
Several se'nnights later

Ella's fingers trembled while she made a second attempt to take needle and thread to the fabric in her hands but 'twas useless as she stared at the knot. Memories of her time with Lady Katherine and the woman's aversion to sewing anything by hand almost had her smiling... almost. But there was nothing about Ella's current situation to smile about, not given the fact that she was living under Simon's roof.

He had been courteous to a fault. Had taken her on outings and even bought her enough fabric from the village that she would have cloth for more than a dozen gowns. Ribbons and baubles had also shown up in her room amongst her things. A small bouquet of wildflowers brightened her table in a vivid display of color in an otherwise stark chamber.

Not that material things were of import, but 'twas nice to be spoiled for a change. She sighed while becoming lost in thought. A person's life and the way they lived it were all that mattered. Simon had gone beyond himself in his attempts to win her heart. He deserved better than what she could offer him.

Simon would no doubt feel betrayed once she bore him the news and she could not delay its telling any longer. She was not sure if she could stand the hurt that would certainly appear upon his face, along with the disappointment that was sure to follow.

She set the fabric down and stood, her hand automatically traveling to her stomach. She was pregnant with Killian's child. With everything that had been going on around her, how had she not thought of when her last monthly courses had occurred? Her fate had somehow changed. Killian would sire a child and he would never know the babe was his.

But Killian was not her immediate problem. How could he be when he did not even know of her in this place in time? Her thoughts went to Simon. She knew how much he cared for her. How would she ever explain to him that she carried another man's baby within her? He would throw her from the gates without haste!

She could no longer put off the inevitable. Wiping the tears she had not even been aware of shedding from her face, she left her bedchamber and made her way to Simon's. He would be surprised to see her at his door but *this* was a conversation to have in private.

Ella went down the darkened passageway and she wished the place had more sconces placed upon the stone walls. If she were to stay, she would have seen that the corridors were properly lit.

She raised her hand to knock upon the closed portal in front of her while a chill swept over her. *Get it over with Ella and let whatever is to happen… happen.* She knocked, and the door was soon opened by a servant who then went back to his master to help him with his cloak.

Simon looked up briefly before taking a ring from the servant who was finishing seeing Simon dressed for the morn.

"Ella, my dearest, I was just about to send someone to your chamber to see if you would care for a stroll by the river. 'Tis a fair clear day," he declared before finally leveling his gaze upon her. "Ella… whatever is the matter?"

"Simon… I must needs have speech with you," she whispered, so softly he leaned forward to hear her.

"Of course," he said before waving to his servant. "Leave us." The man quickly bowed and left, quietly closing the door behind him.

Now that they were alone, Ella was uncertain where to begin. Simon came to her and her knees buckled. He quickly took her about the waist and led her to a chair by the fire. She opened her mouth several times before her lips snapped shut. How she hated to hurt him.

Simon studied her for several moments. "You are leaving me," he finally blurted out reaching for her hands.

"What?" she asked. Did she really hear him say those words or was it just her imagination?

"You wish to leave," he said in a calm flat tone.

"Nay. I do not wish to leave but you may be tossing me from the keep after what I must tell you."

The air rushed from his lungs. "I am relieved."

"Simon..." she gulped and felt a small amount of comfort from the warmth of his hands.

"Tell me what has you so distraught, Ella. We can work through anything as long as we stay together," he declared, his heartfelt declaration almost tore her apart.

"I do not know how to easily say this, and I will pray you will not be angered when I tell you my news." She waited with bated breath while he reached up to run a finger down her cheek, a more loving look she had never seen on his face. "I am pregnant."

His hand dropped and his smile quickly faded. He rose and went to the window to open the shutter. Gripping the edges of stone with white knuckles, he hunched over before he once more stood to full height to stare out silently at the river below.

"I am sorry, Simon," she moaned as she watched the anguish cross what she could see of his face. He wiped at his eyes before turning towards her, his hands clasped behind his back.

"What of the father?"

She thought quickly. There was no sense telling Simon the truth. She did not wish to face the repercussions of him learning of her original roots and possibly end up in the same situation as she had with her son who still needed to be born. "Dead," she whispered, lowering her head with the lie.

"How?"

She raised her eyes to meet his, feeling her own tears on the edges of her lashes. "Does it matter?" Even thinking of Killian as dead made her heart falter. She did not know his fate after he pushed her into the time gate, only that he lived in *this* time at a far younger age, just as she herself was doing.

He sighed, almost as though in defeat. "Nay, I suppose not. Did you love him?"

"Aye, not that such an emotion does either me or the babe any good," she confided. She would *not* denounce the love she felt for her child's father no matter how much she hurt the man in front of her.

He flinched at her admission of loving another. His back remained ramrod straight. "I see."

"I did not mean to hurt you, my lord, and for that I am deeply sorry."

He turned away from her again to stare back through the window. Ella watched him taking several deep breaths as though to gather his composure.

"You must know I care for you, Ella," he muttered as he refused to gaze upon her.

"As I care for you," she answered.

He quickly turned to watch her. "Do you?"

"Aye, how could I not feel an amount of fondness for you, Simon?" She stood to go to him but he held up his hand. She returned to her seat uncertain as to what judgment he would pass upon her.

"But not as much as you loved him," he surmised.

She could not answer him, not when her heart truly belonged to a man she had yet to meet. She had a sense of *déjà vu*. Once she had been sitting in Simon's solar thinking only of Henry. Now here she sat in Simon's bedchamber thinking only of Killian. Had God stepped in and changed her fate yet again? What would such a change do to the future events that must come to pass?

Simon cleared his throat bringing Ella out of her reminiscing. "You do not need to answer my question. I can see for myself such is the case."

"I do not know what to say to ease your suffering."

He came to sit next to her, his hands forming a steeple on the arms of his chair, possibly contemplating their future together. How was she to convince him they should marry while she carried another's babe in her belly? If he tossed her from Hull, Faramond would never be born.

Simon dropped his hands to his lap, fingering one of his rings. "I have a proposal."

"I am listening."

"I am a man who goes after what he wants. You, Ella, are what I want for my wife. I cannot explain why I am acting so rashly after knowing you but a short period of time, but I do know my feelings. I am in love with you even if you carry another man's child."

She gasped for she never thought in her wildest imagination he would utter such words, not given her circumstances. "I do not know what to say, Simon."

"Perchance with time you may one day have a greater amount of affection for me, but I have enough love in my heart to carry me through 'til you do."

"You cannot possibly think we should remain together?"

"Why not? You have a better plan or place to go?" he asked with a raised brow, even though he knew her answer.

"Nay, I do not."

"Mayhap his family will take you in?"

She shook her head. "There is no other place for me to be, other than at Hull."

"Then we will strike a bargain, you and I."

May God help me and give me strength... here come his terms. "Go on."

"We shall wed, posthaste. If you birth a daughter, then I shall claim her as my own. If, however, you have a son, you must know I cannot leave him Hull, not when that would deny my true son his inheritance if we are so blessed. If such is the case, we shall tell them of your husband's death. 'Twill not be hard to convey the truth of the matter. If a girl, no one need ever be the wiser."

"You would allow me to keep my daughter or son and raise the child here?" She was shocked, certain Simon would send her babe to the farthest corner of the earth. He was a prideful man, and this seemed more than she could have thought possible, given their past relationship.

"The child is still yours, Ella, unless you wish to be rid of it. If such is the case, I can make that happen just as easily."

Her arms went protectively around her as if keeping her baby safe. "Nay, I would wish to keep my child no matter if 'tis a boy or girl."

"As long as the child brings you pleasure, then I, too, will be content. Our happiness is all that matters to me."

"You are more than fair, my lord," she replied with a sense of relief 'til their eyes met. He was not done with her as yet.

"There is more."

She nodded. "I expected there would be."

"I never and I repeat *never* wish to know or have you speak *his* name. Is this perfectly clear, *my* lady," he hissed and for the first time Ella was aware of the full extent of his anger hovering just beneath the cool façade he showed her.

"Aye, my lord," she whispered bowing her head in submission, hoping her voice sounded contrite enough to pacify Simon.

"Good! We shall have many happy years ahead of us after the birth of your child."

"I am certain we have much to look forward to, my lord," she agreed.

"We will have many children…"

We will have one son.

"…and if your child is a son, then he and my heir will foster together. I have a distant cousin who has been eager for me to produce a son so he can train him to be a great knight," he beamed, appearing to be pleased with thoughts of his own offspring.

"Nay!" Her voice bounced off the walls and rang in her ears. She knew the outcome of her son in the hands of Simon's cousin. She would never put a child of hers in such danger now that she knew. Not for a second time. A thought whispered across her mind while her brows lifted in surprise. Of course! All her questions were answered, as how she would save her son fell into place.

"You think to gainsay me on this matter?" Simon snapped. "Think again, Ella."

She reached for his hands and, although reluctant, he finally clasped them in his own. "I beseech thee, Simon. Please do not send our son to this man. I know of another place where he will be well taken care of."

He gave her a roguish smile before he pulled her into his lap. She went willingly. After all, she knew he was going to be a good lover and the father to her own child one day. There was no sense putting off the inevitable.

"I like the sound of you speaking of our son, *ma cherie*," he whispered, as though his anger was readily replaced with his need to lay claim to her. "Shall we seal our bargain with a kiss?"

Ella smiled down at her future husband before placing her

lips to his. 'Twas at first gentle, then more demanding when he tightened his arms around her. Simon would be easy to love as long as she could control his temper and the rash decisions he tended to make. Her arms snaked around his neck, fingering the length of his curly hair.

When he finally broke off their kiss, he appeared pleased with the decisions they had agreed between them. "Now… tell me of this place that would be fitting to raise the son of the Lord of Hull," he encouraged.

Ella smiled in delight, knowing her children's future would be safe. "There is a place in the north called Berwyck…"

Months later, Ella gave birth to a healthy son with brown hair with reddish hues. His eyes were blue-green and a replica of his father's, not that the lady ever told that to the Lord of Hull. They named him Conrad.

Although Simon had sworn he would be indifferent if the child was male, he still rejoiced at the arrival of Ella's son. Upon his birth, Simon took the babe to the window and held the infant up so his people could see their child and also welcome him to the world.

And far to the north, a certain Scotsman suddenly halted the swing of his sword while training on the lists with his laird. He knew not what had caused his hesitation, but knew something in the world as he knew it had shifted. The thought was fleeting and left his mind just as quickly as it had entered before he returned to what he was doing… an attempt to best his laird upon the lists.

Two years later, after a difficult birthing, Ella produced Hull's heir. This child also resembled *his* father with his dark black hair and grey eyes. Her husband was so pleased, he opened the doors of the castle in a celebration that lasted nigh unto a se'nnight. The boy was named Faramond and, unknowingly to the child as he grew, his fate had been changed.

CHAPTER 29

Berwyck Castle
The Year of Our Lord's Grace 1164

Killian opened the stable door, peering carefully into the dimly lit interior for there was danger afoot this day! In his hands he held forth a wooden sword. Waving the makeshift weapon in front of him, he entered to stand in the middle of the room. Where were they?

A howl rang from the rafters, causing Killian to raise his eyes in fear when he saw a young lad swinging on a rope from the upper loft. Good Lord, his laird would have his head if the boy killed himself while in his care.

Holding out his arms he was prepared to catch the boy but before he could get a grasp on the lad, another bellow reached his ears from behind. The young scamps had planned a front and rear attack at the same time to catch him off guard. Well done!

The boy landed on his back while the other bairn attached himself to his leg... or was it the girl. 'Twas hard to determine, since they were both dressed as lads. The Lady Catherine would have a fit when she learned her daughter had been dressing thusly yet again.

'Twas hard not to laugh, but Killian held back his chuckle not wishing to injure the bairn's pride. Aye, they were full of themselves and their ability to stand together as though one instead of two individuals.

He grabbed at the child at his back and held the scamp before him. A boyish guffaw escaped the lad. Aiden stared back at Killian with mischievous violet eyes.

"Get the nasty beastie, Amiria," the boy called out to his sister.

Killian grunted when the lass bit the calf of his leg. This had gone far enough!

He tucked Aiden beneath one arm while his free hand grabbed at Amiria's tunic. He held the squirming bairn before him, inspecting her from the top of her flaming red hair down to her boots.

"Bitin'? A knight of the realm dinnae resort tae such a tactic, lassie," he scowled at the wee girl before giving her a bit of a shake.

"How else was I tae best ye, Uncle Killian," Amiria said. There was such a serious expression on her young face his lips twitched.

Uncle... The word was meant with the utmost respect, although Killian knew they were not related by blood, other than belonging to the same clan. 'Twas a grim reminder he had yet to take a wife and sire a child, although the twins were more than enough for any one man to guard or handle. They were forever getting into one scrap or another whether with themselves or with their younger sister, Sabina.

"Ye seem tae know much for all yer... what... eight summers?" he asked, knowing full well their age. He set them both down to stand before him while he folded his arms across his chest to intimidate them.

They placed their hands upon their hips. "Ye know we are nine summers, Killian," they said in unison then turned to one another. A peal of laugher leaked from their lips 'til they fell to the floor with their own jest. 'Twas a common occurrence for them to speak the same words or finish each other's thoughts.

Mirth wracked Killian's chest 'til he, too, laughed alongside the twins. He squatted down and picked up one of the wooden swords that had fallen to the floor in their efforts to get the better of him. He gave them each a playful poke 'til they looked upon him with a blank expression as though they had done no wrong.

"What am I tae do with the two of ye?" Killian asked, as they leaned on their elbows staring back at him.

Aiden quickly stood. "Train us, Uncle Killian."

"Aye. Train us tae be a mighty warrior just like ye are, Uncle," Amiria said agreeing with her twin when she, too, stood next to her brother.

"Bah!" Killian replied. "Ye are too young for that."

Aiden puffed out his chest. "I am not," he replied looking down at his sister. Although twins, he was already slightly taller than the lass and she did not care for difference in height one bit. "Why I should have already left to be a page at some other castle. Father said so, even though Mother told him nay."

Amiria gasped. "Ye canna leave me, Aiden," she cried out before she threw herself into his arms. They held onto one another before they appeared to recover themselves. Shuffling their feet, they peeked at one another shyly as though 'twas unseemly for them to share an affection between them that only twins could understand.

Killian stood and placed an arm around each of their shoulders. "Someday, Aiden, ye will be a great knight like yer father," he predicted. "Ye will have the responsibility of being laird of the clan and taking care of our people."

Amiria looked up at him with big eyes. "What of me, Killian? Will I be a great knight too?"

The poor wee lamb, Killian thought, knowing her lot in life would most likely lead her to being the wife of a Scottish laird at some distant castle. Laird Douglas would only want the best for his daughter.

He pulled Amiria to his side in a brief hug before he let her go to open the stable door for them to pass. "Ye shall be a fine lady, like yer mother."

The lass stomped her foot. "But I wish tae be a knight!" she fumed.

Aiden gave her a push causing her to stumble through the door. "Ye cannae be a knight," he teased, following her out into the sunlight. "Ye be a girl."

Amiria let out a squeal of protest before rushing to her brother. Wrapping her arms around his waist she tackled him into the dirt. Fists began to fly and Killian entered the fray to pull the two apart but not before another had something to say on the matter.

"Aiden! Amiria!" their names being called out by their sire had them placing their hands behind their backs but not before they stuck their tongue's out at one another.

Killian looked up to see the laird and lady of the castle

greeting guests. A knight was descending from his saddle; two lads sat on their ponies while a woman waited in a wagon with her attendants. He assumed 'twas the wife and mother to the two boys. She was heavily garbed, a thick veil covering her head. He briefly pondered if she was mayhap one of those pious women who did her duty to her husband but devoted her life to God. 'Twas none of his concern, in either case.

Lady Catherine excused herself and made her way to Killian and her disobedient children. She wagged a finger at the twins.

"You embarrass me and your father in front of guests?" she accused while the bairns had the decency to look down.

"Sorry, Mother," they replied.

"Get to the keep and clean yourselves up this instant," she scolded, before she took hold of Amiria's tunic. "And you, young lady, will don clothes that befit your station in life. You are the daughter of the Laird of Berwyck. Do *not* let me see you in hose and tunic again!"

"Aye, Mother," Amiria whispered, her eyes filling with unshed tears. She took the back of her hand to wipe her face before glancing at Killian. He nodded towards the keep in a silent demand to do as she was told.

"I appreciate you looking after them, Killian," Lady Catherine said while placing her hand in the crook of his elbow. "I know they can be a trial."

"'Tis an honor tae be entrusted with their care, my lady," Killian replied, glancing toward the new arrivals.

"I fear Amiria will never conform to being a lass unless Douglas does something about allowing her to play with her wooden sword."

"They are just bairns, Lady Catherine." Killian answered, before pointing towards the group who awaited the lady's return. He watched when the lady across the bailey descended from the wagon. "Who are they?"

"Come and let me introduce you to the Lord and Lady of Hull. They have brought their sons to foster here."

"They appear too young tae be squires," Killian replied.

"Conrad, the oldest, is ten summers and Faramond eight. Douglas has insisted we take the boys on. I would not gainsay him."

They began walking towards the couple and he watched while the woman moved behind her husband and sons while introductions began. He could not fully see her face and yet, when their eyes met, Killian swore he knew her. *What the bloody hell?*

CHAPTER 30

Ella held onto the back of Simon's surcoat for dear life. *My God! There he is.* She knew she would eventually see Killian here but she thought mayhap she could venture to Berwyck without this chance encounter. She needed to remain unseen, an obscure face in a chance meeting that would leave no memory in his mind.

Simon attempted to pull her forward. "Whatever is the matter, dear?" he asked, concern etched upon his features.

"I fear I am unwell. The travel…" her voice, hoarse in her own ears, trailed off. She could not take her eyes from Killian, although she knew she should. He was so young… so incredibly handsome with his broad shoulders and brownish-red hair with no hint of grey like she remembered. He looked upon her as a complete stranger, which broke her heart all over again. Time seemed to be playing tricks with her mind for she could not in all honestly work out how many years it had now been since she had last seen Killian.

Simon nodded. "Mayhap we may see to my lady wife and she can be shown to a chamber to rest. She has never been one to easily endure a journey over a great distance."

Laird Douglas nodded but 'twas Lady Catherine who spoke first. "But of course. Please follow me."

Ella was going to faint. She just knew when she had to pass by Killian she was going to land at his feet in a heap, and how the hell was she to explain such a happening? But she somehow managed to stay upright. She kept her head down, the veil becoming a shield hiding her face to the best of her ability.

She could not let the inhabitants of Berwyck become familiar with her. She had but one task… to see her sons to Berwyck and then get out as quickly as possible. She would feign sickness and the need to be at her prayers as an excuse to stay inside the chamber she was to be given.

She had been to this keep before, albeit a decade or more from now, and mayhap all would be well. The lord and lady were unknown to her, although she hated the thought of Amiria's parents being dead in the future. Ella began to wonder just how old Amiria was. She started ticking off the years inside her head while she continued following Lady Catherine into the keep and up the turret stairs.

"I hate ye both," a child screamed, running down the fourth floor passageway.

Ella barely moved out of the way before a child threw herself into her mother's body.

"There, there now, Sabina. Whatever is the matter?" Catherine said soothing the lass by leaning down and hugging her.

Sabina… the third child of the lord and lady of Berwyck and probably no more than seven summers, Ella supposed. Sabina would one day be a handful and end up being abused as no woman would ever wish. She had joined a nunnery after her ordeal, much to Amiria's dismay. Ella wondered if the girl had ever taken her vows.

The child sobbed again. "They be so mean to me, Mother. They put mud in my new shoes."

"I see," Catherine replied. She stood and kept her arm around the lass. "We shall see if they can be cleaned and if not, I shall get you another pair."

"You will?"

"Aye, of course, sweetling."

"What about Aiden and Amir—"

Lady Catherine gazed at Ella with a patient smile. "I will deal with the twins. Off you go. I need to see the Lady of Hull to a chamber so she may rest."

Ella watched the young girl skip down the passageway before she disappeared from view. "You have twins?" Ella inquired, as though she was not privy to such information.

"Aye, and another daughter, Lynet, who is but four summers. The twins are a handful and most mischievous. I never know what they shall do next."

Ella smiled, happy to meet Amiria's mother. "Children will be children."

Catherine chuckled. "Aye, you have that aright. You have two fine boys as well. Are they close?"

"They are my pride and joy, Lady Catherine. Conrad and Faramond get along well enough… they are brothers after all, and much like your own children, they have their moments."

"I only wish I could get my Amiria to act like a girl instead of following her brother into one scrap or another. The lass will be the death of me, I swear," Catherine said, coming to a door and opening it. She motioned to a servant who was leaving another chamber and pointed inside. No orders were given. 'Twas as though the woman knew what was expected of her. The fire was banked, the coverlet turned down on the bed before she left just as quietly as she had entered.

When the lady motioned for Ella to enter, she was about to step inside the chamber but paused briefly at the threshold. Did this lady have some inner knowledge that this exact room would be the one Ella would be given whenever she ventured to Berwyck? She raised a questioning brow to Lady Catherine who only smiled, strode across the room to take up a pitcher and pour a chalice of wine.

"You must be parched after your trip. I hope you will be comfortable here while you remain at Berwyck," she said, holding out her offering to Ella, who took it in trembling hands.

"We will not stay long," Ella replied, her nerves rattled in her body. "Only long enough to rest our horses so we can then return to Hull."

"Aye, I know," Catherine murmured with a strange smile.

"You do?"

The woman nodded before reaching over to squeeze Ella's numb hand. Catherine pulled her over to a chair near the hearth and Ella fell into it before her knees gave out.

"Our healer Shona *sees* many things and tells me of her visions if she feels they are of import. Her daughter, Kenna, has the same gift, although she is but a child of eleven summers," Catherine replied. "I believe you will one day meet her on your return travels to Berwyck."

"Aye..." Ella whispered not daring to say more.

"Your secret is safe with me," Catherine said as if to calm

Ella's fears, "and your sons will be well taken care of. Douglas will see to Faramond's training. Killian, to Conrad's."

"I do not know how to thank you, my lady. You have lifted a great weight from my shoulders," Ella replied, humbly grateful to this kind woman.

Lady Catherine went to the door. Before she opened it, she turned to once more stare at Ella. The woman's eyes sparkled with unshed tears "Perchance you can return the favor one day and look after my children, though they may be grown by the time you next return. They will need a mother figure in their lives considering what is to come."

Ella could only stare in wonder that the lady before her could stand there so calmly while she sputtered on about future events, including her own demise. "'Twould be my privilege, Lady Catherine."

Relief swept across the lady's visage as she mumbled her thanks and quit the room, leaving Ella in a daze. She and Simon needed to get the hell out of Berwyck and fast!

※

A se'nnight later, Killian watched as horses were readied in the outer bailey along with the wagon prepared to carry the Lady of Hull on her return trip home. Her sons stood near their father who was whispering to the boys, most likely telling them to behave.

Killian shivered, but 'twas not from the cold. He felt *her* draw near and something inside his heart lurched when she came to stand beside him. He peered down upon her while a frown crossed his brow. He searched his mind for where he may have seen the lady before, but no memory came to him.

Her voice, a sweet tinkling melody to his ears, caused his hands to tremble. "You will take good care of our son," she murmured.

"Aye," Killian said having already been told he was to teach the boys all he knew, especially the eldest, Conrad. "Laird Douglas is a fair lord. Ye and Lord Simon have no reason tae fear for them. They will be well seen tae and lack for nothing."

The lady pulled her gaze from her boys to stare upon Killian who staggered backwards. She held her veil over the lower portion of her face, revealing nothing of her visage but her eyes and yet he *knew* this woman! How the devil did he know of her?

"I pray you will one day forgive me… Killian…" His name, a mere whisper in the wind, lingered between them.

"Forgive ye for what, milady?" he asked, his brows furrowed while pondering why she must ask his forgiveness.

He received no answer, for she left him standing there alone. He observed the lady taking both boys aside, giving them each a fierce hug before the lads began to fuss, most likely not wishing to be seen with their mother coddling them. A sob was torn from the lady's lips as her husband assisted her into the wagon. A portion of a tarp or makeshift curtain dropped and the lady disappeared within. Her cries of anguish tore at Killian's heart.

Lord Simon made excuses for his distraught wife before once more thanking Laird Douglas for taking in his sons. With a wave of farewell, their party left the bailey and made their way through the barbican gate disappearing from view.

Killian stood there, fretting over the woman's words while watching the dust settle after their departure.

"She is a nice lady," a young voice said standing next to him.

Killian gazed down to stare at Mistress Shona's daughter, Kenna. The girl's hair was as black as the midnight skies, her eyes as green as the Scottish moors. She held the hand of the little lass, Lynet, whose hair was blonde with eyes as blue as the sky above them. They were the opposite of each other and yet Kenna tended to look after the laird's youngest MacLaren daughter at only four summers.

"Do ye know of her?" Killian asked, doubtful the child had spent much time with the Lady of Hull. He had not seen much of her during her brief time at Berwyck, as she preferred to stay in her chamber and remain at her prayers, or so he had been told.

Kenna's laughter rang out in the morning air. "O' course I know her, Killian as do ye. How could ye ever forget Ella?" she answered, before tugging Lynet by the hand and heading toward the garden.

Ella... something altered inside Killian once he thought on the woman's name. He should know her name *and* her face, should he not? But there was no time to ponder where he met the Lady of Hull. Not when the laird of the clan called the men to the lists, nor when he began showing Conrad and Faramond the castle grounds and the place they would call home for many a year.

Ella... he would ponder *her* on another day.

※

Two years later, Berwyck castle would have but one day to rejoice over the birth of their laird's next son, Patrick. For 'twas the fate of the Lady Catherine that she did not recover after the lad's delivery and died but two days later, plunging the inhabitants of the castle into mourning.

'Twas but a foreshadowing of other events yet to come...

CHAPTER 31

Berwyck Castle
The Year of Our Lord's Grace 1170

The training field rang out with the sound of metal clashing upon metal. Laird Douglas and Killian stood on the side watching the knights in their skirmishes. As Killian looked upon the field, he shook his head, seeing only young children practicing. What was coming over Berwyck these days?

Conrad and Faramond were holding their own and Killian watched them with a fierce sense of pride while they hacked away at each other. And why not? He had practically raised them and Conrad was almost a grown man at ten and six summers. Although their sire had traveled to Berwyck upon occasion, their mother never returned. *'Twas probably for the best*, he thought, although why the woman continued to trouble him remained a mystery. He returned his gaze to the field.

The mournful sounds of the bagpipe echoed in the cool morning air while the clan's piper taught his son Garrick, who was aged ten and six summers, the notes to keep the men moving at their paces. Aiden was off to the side practicing with bow and arrow, and cheers of encouragement rang out when he hit the center of his target.

But 'twas the laird's daughter Amiria who held his interest while she fought with a young man who had shown up recently at Berwyck's gate seeking refuge. Ian MacGillivray was ten and nine summers and had grimaced when the laird had partnered Ian with his daughter. Still… she was holding up well against a knight who was full of himself and ready to prove his worth to the world.

Laird Douglas chuckled while he watched his daughter. "She fights like she was born with a sword in her hand," he said proudly. "Where has the time gone that my oldest bairns are already ten and five summers? I am starting to feel my age."

A snort escaped Killian while he also pondered when time had seemingly passed them by. "Yer lady wouldnae have approved," he answered tugging at his beard while he concentrated on the bairns.

Douglas chuckled. "I am not so certain of that, Killian."

"I must point out they sound more like yer wife, God rest her soul, than they do ye, my laird."

A grunt left Douglas while he, too, perused the group. "Aye… even Ian and Thomas could pass for English like my beloved Catherine, unless ye anger them. 'Tis when their Scottish accent gives them away. But I wouldnae deprive them of my wife's company and she enjoyed having them about and under her care."

"But ye are right in one aspect. Yer wee lass was born tae fight and not be stuck in a solar with the women."

They watched when Thomas Kincaid, who had come to Berwyck prior to Lady Catherine's death after the youngest bairn Patrick was born, stepped onto the field and advanced towards the pair. After his sire had disowned the lad, Thomas had become part of the MacLaren clan, since he was a distant relation. He had even been given his own chamber within the castle keep proving to all he was considered family.

Killian held his breath when Thomas and Ian, who were but a year apart, gave each other a salute then turned as one with cocky grins towards their young opponent.

"So… you think you can best me," Amiria taunted, brandishing her sword. "Let us see who lands in the dirt first, shall we?"

"Mayhap ye should stop this, my laird," Killian suggested.

"She shall hold her own, never fear, Killian," Douglas replied with a wink of conspiracy. "She is, after all, my daughter."

"If ye say so, but I wouldnae trust those two. I can see they are out tae teach the lass a lesson."

Douglas turned his full attention to Killian. "Ye dinnae have faith in them?"

"'Tis not that. Mayhap they remind me too much of myself at such an age," Killian replied.

Douglas nodded. "I have watched them carefully for some time now. Ian and Thomas have been nothing but honorable while here at Berwyck. I would trust them with my life and that of my children. 'Tis the reason I made Ian captain of Amiria's guard. He is young but devoted tae her. I also have hope tae have Thomas as one of her guardsmen."

"I, too, would trust either man tae watch my back. 'Tis only they appear as if they wish tae put Lady Amiria in her place. I fear for her."

Douglas nodded. "Never let her know ye fear for her, Killian. She and Adrian have more pride in their hearts than most men I know, and Amiria makes every effort tae prove she is as good with a sword as her brother."

A howl of pain rang out when Amiria slammed her elbow into Thomas's stomach when he swung his sword wide. She took the advantage by ducking under his arm and giving him a mighty push. He may not have landed in the dirt but he stumbled all the same.

"Ha! I bested you, Thomas! Admit it," Amiria called out. Her mistake was to turn her back on Ian who promptly yanked on her tunic. She fell backwards into his chest to find a dirk at her throat.

Ian chuckled. "Never turn away from your enemy, Amiria, lest you wish to see your life cut short." He let the blade fall when she turned in his arms.

"But I have you to guard my back, my captain," she smirked with violet eyes sparkling, causing Ian to laugh.

He pointed the blade at Amiria. "Remember the lesson, little one," Ian replied before reaching down to hide the weapon in his boot.

Killian sighed in relief while witnessing the scene, but it was short lived when he saw the wee lass Lynet racing across the list, dodging the knights who barely had time to stop their training when she ran by them.

"Ian! Ian!" She called out, her blonde hair flying out behind her.

"*God's Bone's,* she is going tae be killed," Douglas managed before he yelled out to his men to cease their training.

The youngster had no notion as to the ruckus she had caused before she made her way to Ian. Killian and Douglas came up behind her wondering what was so important.

"I finished this for you, Ian," Lynet said, her blue eyes shining with happiness.

Ian put away his sword to kneel down before the young girl who was now but a mere ten summers. "And what is it you have accomplished, my lady?" he asked.

"Why, I have made you a favor for your arm, sir knight. See here how the thread matches your hazel eyes?" she murmured, showing him the ribbon she had sewn for him.

'Twas far from perfect, but Killian could see she took great pride in her needlework and he wondered what Ian would do next. He did not have long to wait for the answer.

"You made this for me?" he asked, while his lips curved into a pleased smile.

Lynet nodded and held out the ribbon. "Aye... will you wear my colors, Ian, and always remember me?"

Ian held out his arm so the girl could tie the favor upon his arm. "You show me a great honor, Lady Lynet. 'Tis a privilege to have you bestow upon me my first favor."

"Truly?" she gasped. "No other lady has given you one to wear on your arm as you go into battle?"

"Nary a one. Thank you, my lady," he said and took her hand to bestow a kiss above her knuckles, ignoring the sniggering of the knights who had stopped to watch the laird's youngest daughter making a scene before the well-trained men.

Lynet twirled around in happiness as though the stars had shined down upon her to give a hint of what might occur one day between them. Her joy was short lived, however, when her sire gave her a fierce frown, ordering her back to the keep and the men to return to their training.

They had no more time to contemplate the goings on with the MacLaren bairns, for a servant came running up to Laird Douglas with a missive. He perused it quickly before turning the parchment over to Killian to read.

"Lord Simon is dead," Killian read.

"Aye," Douglas said, "and his sons need tae be told. They must return tae Hull."

"It does not say how he perished."

Douglas turned to him. "Does it matter?"

"Nay, I suppose not. I wonder how his lady is holding up after the death of her husband?"

"Ye shall find out for yerself when ye deliver the lads tae their home," Douglas ordered.

"Why me?" Killian asked not sure how he felt about seeing the woman who haunted him these many years.

"Who else would I trust tae deliver the Lady of Hull's sons tae see their sire before he is buried?" Douglas asked. "Besides, ye are close tae them both and I know first-hand they hold ye in the deepest respect. Why, ye are like a second father to them."

"If this is what ye ask of me, then I shall see the lads home."

That very eve, dreams began to invade Killian's slumber. Conversations swam inside his head he knew had never taken place with the Lady of Hull. More troubling was the vision of the woman, whose face was clearly revealed when she had never shown her visage to him before. He took the lady in his arms and made love to her in a forest as they declared their love to one another. 'Twas as though the dream was in fact a memory that had been hidden away inside his mind for years, and only now was revealed for him to remember all they had meant to one another.

With a heavy heart, Killian left Berwyck to deliver Conrad and Faramond home to their mother the next morn. He was uneasy and he did not fully understand why. What did fate have him store for him and why, of a sudden, did he feel the need to have Lady Ella near his side?

CHAPTER 32

Hull Castle

Ella sat in her hall, exhaustion riddling her body 'til she could longer think straight. She gave a nod in acknowledgment when another of the villagers came to pay their respect to her late husband then left. *Simon...* he was gone from this life and had hopefully found peace in the next one. At least this time around he was not accused of treason with his head lopped off by an angry king.

But the illness that had consumed his body was not necessarily a better way to go and 'twas not as though Ella had the advantage of modern medicine to heal the man. She had wished she could have given him the medicine she knew would have been necessary centuries from now in order for him to recover. The way he had labored in his attempt to breathe made Ella assume he had pneumonia and she watched with a sense of helplessness when Simon grew worse. She made every attempt to persuade him to drink plenty of fluids but 'twas not enough and he finally succumbed to his illness and passed from this world.

"*Did you love me at all, Ella...*" he had whispered that last night while she sat at his bedside holding his hand.

"*Aye, Simon, and I love you still,*" she had answered truthfully, for she did love her husband, to the best she was capable of loving him when her heart still belonged to another. He had always known such had been the case from the very beginning and at least that one aspect of their relationship had not changed. What mattered the most was to give him what comfort she was capable of. She had saved both her sons. She only wished she could have saved her husband from his fate, too.

Was it a sin to still love Killian or was it worse to betray that love by marrying Simon? she mused. Simon's last words still haunted her and mayhap they would echo inside her memories for years to come. *Time was a bitch...* the modern phrase flitted through her head while she pondered how many more years would pass before she could meet up with Killian on the beach near Berwyck. Her estimate was twelve but, 'til then, there was still more she needed to accomplish. There was still the happiness of others at stake if she failed.

The door to the keep opened yet again and a sob tore through Ella's lips to witness her sons standing across the room. She fell to the floor, opening her arms wide. *Her sons were home! My... just look at how they had grown in their absence from her life.*

"Mother!" They called out to her and ran across the hall before throwing themselves into her waiting arms.

Ella at last held them at arm's length, cupping each of their cheeks before wiping at their tears. "Let me look at you… What handsome young men you are becoming," she beamed.

"F-father?" Faramond stammered and Ella nodded to their sire laid out in front of the hearth.

"He loved you both," she told them while she watched unshed tears gather in their eyes. "Go pay your respects."

She watched her youngest son leave her side but turned to Conrad who remained. *My God! Could not Killian see for himself that this young man was the spitting image of him?*

"How are you, mother?" Conrad asked, a worried frown marring his otherwise handsome young face.

"As well as can be expected. You have been treated fairly at Berwyck?"

"Aye. They treat us as though we are family. I suppose Faramond must stay here now that he is Lord of Hull." Conrad folded his arms across his chest and Ella's heart squeezed tight.

"Aye. You can stay, too," she said fearing his answer. "Hull is also your home."

Conrad gave her a sad sort of smile. "It has never been my home, mother," he replied quietly. "You are what made this place bearable. How can I stay here knowing I would be but a vassal to my younger brother?"

"You are still kin despite having different fathers."

"Since my true sire is dead, I need to make my own way in the world, mother. Surely you can understand the circumstances for what they are?"

Ella reached out for his hand. "Will not your situation be the same at Berwyck?"

He shrugged. "I seem to belong there. The clan and people have accepted me like I am one of their own. Lord Douglas is reasonable and Killian has more or less taken me, and Faramond for that matter, under his wing. There is much I can still learn under his tutelage."

"Killian?" she whispered before slipping down into her chair. The last thing she needed was to faint in a dead heap at Conrad's feet.

"Aye. He brought us here but, with your permission, I would like to return with him to Berwyck." He went to her side to kneel by her feet.

"Killian is here?" Her question lingered on her lips as all the blood rushed from her face.

"Aye. Mother… Are you certain you are well? You look pale," Conrad asked in concern.

"I am not sure," she murmured.

Ella clutched Conrad's hand in an attempt to halt the world from spinning out of control. But her fate tumbled wildly out of any sense of finding stability, especially when the door to her hall opened. Killian filled the portal as though she had wished him to appear. There was no place for her to hide. He had seen her face… the one thing she had attempted to keep from him was fully exposed. She gasped, swiftly wondering if he now recognized her and how much he remembered of their time together in their future lives. God help her!

※

Killian swayed and clutched at the frame of the door to steady himself. Images of the Lady of Hull… Ella, *his* Ella in some other place in time, swirled in his mind. Some of the images made no sense, but the one from his dream just nights before made him realize he *knew* this woman as surely as he knew he would draw his next breath.

He straightened himself, pulling down on his tunic before making his way across the room. Mistress Shona's words rang clearly in his head, a grim reminder he was not to let Ella know that they had been acquainted, for she had other tasks she must complete before they could be together.

He bowed before the pale lady. "My deepest condolences on the loss of yer husband, my lady," he said. His voice was calm when he was anything but composed.

"You are too kind, Sir Killian, to bring my boys back to Hull so they may pay their final respect to their sire. I hope your journey was without difficulty?"

"'Twas without incident."

She waved her hand towards her son who stood next to her, his hand resting upon her shoulder. "Conrad tells me he wishes to return with you to Berwyck," she said raising her eyes to her son. "I assume he will continue to be welcome there amongst the people and their laird?"

Killian gaze swept over the lad. He was so proud of the young man Conrad was becoming; a well-trained knight anyone would be grateful to call their son. A moment of regret flashed in his mind that he would never sire a bairn of his own.

"Sir Killian?" Lady Ella called, bringing him back from his sudden melancholy mood.

"Aye... Conrad is well received amongst the people of Berwyck and will be most welcome tae return tae live there," he answered, with a nod to Conrad who returned his gesture with a nod of his own.

"Then I shall leave him once more in your care. I understand

Conrad feels there is more you can teach him and he is looking forward to the training," the lady replied, giving her son's hand a squeeze.

"Does he now?" Killian chuckled, folding his arms over his chest. "He may regret such an admission once he returns tae the lists."

Conrad leaned down. "Mother, you are embarrassing me."

"Bah! I am doing no such thing. Besides, we are all like extended family, are we not?" she replied while returning her gaze to Killian.

Their gazes locked and Killian had the sudden urge to sweep this woman up into his arms and kiss her senseless. But now was not the time. Not when her dead husband was laid out in her hall and the sound of Faramond's tears reached his ears.

"Aye… like family. I will take good care of Conrad while he is in my care, my lady."

"See that you do, Sir Killian, or you shall be answering to me," Ella stated firmly.

He bowed before her. "If I may pay my respects and see tae Faramond?" Killian asked while motioning to the front of the hall."

"But of course," the lady replied. "Conrad… go with Sir Killian and see to your brother. I am certain he is in need of you. If you will excuse me, the day has been trying and I will take my ease in my chamber. A room will be readied for your stay, Sir Killian."

Before Killian could form a reply, the lady left the hall even though his eyes never left her 'til she disappeared from view. He could ponder the woman no longer… her sons called for him and he could do nothing but go to their side to ease their suffering.

A se'nnight later, Killian and Conrad left Hull. The last words Ella said to him were once more to take care of her son. But that was not what troubled him the most. Aye, 'twas not hard to watch over a young man who meant all to Killian. Far more troubling were her whispered words that war was coming.

CHAPTER 33

The Siege of Berwyck
The Year of Our Lord's Grace 1174

Killian swung his sword as though his life was dependent on keeping the blade in motion, which it was. He was unsure how many more knights would be felled by his hand before the madness would cease. But a look at the field told him the carnage was not over. Not many could win a battle against Henry II's most seasoned warrior, Dristan, the Devil's Dragon of Blackmore, and the clan's numbers were unfortunately dwindling from the onslaught. If his laird did not yield the day, the clan would be wiped out of existence by an invading army who came only to conquer in the name of their king.

Killian spat in the dirt before taking on his next adversary, his mind consumed with the need to survive the onslaught at their gates. 'Twas obvious Berwyck would fall to the English once more, and any thoughts his laird may have had of peace between England and Scotland vanished the moment the Devil's Dragon's army set foot upon their land. Negotiations had been brief and Douglas had refused the terms Dristan of Blackmore all but ordered for Douglas's surrender.

"Get Amiria to the keep," his laird bellowed, and Killian was momentarily confused 'til he saw for himself the small knight in the distance he thought was Aiden was in fact the lass. *God's Blood! What the bloody hell was she doing upon the battlefield?*

Killian continued hacking away at a path to get near to Amiria. The barbican gate had already been breached; the outer bailey was about to be lost as well. If they did not get the twins inside the keep, the enemy could possibly capture them and that would ensure the laird gave up his attempt to keep Berwyck with the Scots.

"Ian," Killian yelled. "Get Amiria tae the keep while I get tae Aiden."

Killian watched in satisfaction when Ian began pulling Amiria towards the castle while the young woman cursed him to the very devil. But Ian had strength on his side, which was something Amiria could in no way overcome. Killian was unprepared to see them pause in their quest to reach safety. Killian swiveled to find what had riveted their attention.

"Father!" Amiria's scream tore across Killian's heart when he saw Douglas's body begin to fall, a sword from his opponent being removed quickly from his body. No sooner had Killian observed this horror than he was next witnessing Aiden falling nearby as he made an attempt to rush to his father's aid.

"Aiden! No!" Amiria was squirming to be released from Ian's grasp. "Let me go, Ian. I must save them."

Killian pointed his sword towards the inner bailey. "Get her the hell out of here, Ian. Now! 'Tis an order!"

Killian raced to reach Douglas's side, killing the knight who had felled his laird. He swiftly knelt to remove Douglas's helmet and was amazed at the strength in Douglas's grip when he pulled at Killian's tabard.

"Promise me ye shall see my bairns safe," Douglas managed to order him, while a small trail of blood leaked from the corner of his mouth.

"We will get ye inside tae safety, my laird," Killian said instead.

"Promise me," Douglas growled out. "Get tae Aiden and see him tae the outskirts of the farthest village on Berwyck's land. No one must know he yet lives, not even his sister. I willnae have my son captured by the Devil's Dragon."

"I give ye my word, my laird," Killian whispered as Douglas's eyes closed.

Though his laird was still breathing, he tore himself from Douglas's side and ran to Aiden's. Conrad was already kneeling by the young man and Killian knew he must send Conrad away to ensure he, too, would be safe.

"Richard," Killian called to one of Berwyck's most trusted knights. When the man was able to make his way to Killian's side, he gave his orders. "Conrad, ye will go with Richard and several other knights and see Aiden to an outlying village for him to heal from his injuries. He cannae be taken by the enemy at any cost. Do what ye can for him to ease his suffering but get yerself through the postern gate to safety."

"I cannot leave you, Killian," Conrad protested, before quickly standing to thrust his sword into a knight who came to attack Killian from behind. Conrad returned just as swiftly but stood guard over Aiden. "What will become of you and those who yet live of the clan?"

Killian stood, a hand resting on Conrad's shoulder. "Berwyck is lost, lad," he said, while sorrow wracked his heart. "I willnae lose ye, too. See Aiden tae safety then get yerself to Hull. 'Tis already under England's rule and should keep ye safe and out of harm's way."

"But what of you?" Conrad attempted once more.

"I must see tae the bairns tae ensure they remain safe."

"Yet you expect me to flee from my duties? To run away like a coward?" Conrad fumed.

Killian began swiftly walking while Richard and another knight took Aiden's unresponsive body. They reached the inner bailey and Killian ordered the gate shut. "Ye are hardly a coward. I ask ye tae protect the heir of Berwyck and see him, and yerself, tae safety. Ye are not running away."

"Killian, I cannot leave you."

He pulled the young man around the corner of the healers' hut, holding him at arm's length before crushing him into his arms. "Ye are like the son I never had, Conrad. No man could be prouder of ye than I am. But yer mother will have my hide if ye are put in any more danger than ye have already experienced. Save Aiden, tell no one he is alive, then get yerself tae Hull. As soon as I am able, I will come tae see ye there. Now, go!"

Killian gave Conrad no further chance to argue with him as he gave him a push in the direction of the postern gate. He sadly watched the young man leave before turning back to his duties to the clan.

"Fall back! Fall back tae the keep," he yelled, running towards the front of the castle.

He took one last look at the empty courtyard as the last of the clansmen took whatever meager belongings they carried inside the castle. Killian bounded up the steps. Once inside, several knights lifted a heavy wooden plank across the door. He stared at the barrier knowing that it, too, would be breached in matter of time.

He took surveillance of the great hall, a grim look crossing his features when he saw what remained of Clan MacLaren. 'Twas then he came upon three of his laird's bairn, huddled near their father's chair by the massive hearth. Killian made quick work of crossing the distance to reach them.

"Sabina! Lynet! Patrick!" he called out, his arm waving for them to quickly follow. He ushered the siblings toward the turret stairs where Thomas and Finlay of Amiria's guardsmen stood at attention. "Get them tae their mother's solar and protect them. Let no one enter. Is this understood?" he commanded.

"Aye, Killian," they replied in unison while taking the children by their hands to ascend the stairs.

Killian had no more time to ponder the safety of the youngsters, for a loud boom was heard as the door to the keep was hit with a massive weight. Killian formed a line of defense with the rest of the clansmen who yet lived. God be merciful that they might survive what was yet to come.

CHAPTER 34

Hull
January 1175

Ella pulled at the shawl wrapped around her shoulders bringing the edges closer together. Huddled near the fire in her solar, she sought the warmth of the flames to ease the cold from her numb body. For months she had waited for Killian to return for Conrad, both eager for his return and dreading it at the same time. This waiting for them to at last be together was getting the best of her and, as the years passed, she was just as anxious now as she was when she had been looking forward to her reunion with Henry.

Her memory of Conrad stumbling into the keep months ago still haunted her. She praised God her son yet lived and that Killian had also survived the siege at Berwyck's gates a second time. Her son was over a score of years now and each day she passed in his company he reminded Ella more and more of

Killian. The man must surely be blind not to see the resemblance between them. Anyone with eyes in their head should have recognized they were related.

She gazed upon her outstretched hands wondering when they had started to age. Forty-seven years was old for this century, though merely middle aged in her birth century. A heavy sigh escaped her and she shook her head as if that alone would take her out of her sudden melancholy mood. With Conrad and Faramond gone to London to appease the king's demand they attend court, Ella had been left to suffer her own company and her mood continued to sour at their absence. Her memories haunted her waking hours as she continued to fret about what harm she may have caused when she altered her future. Since Faramond loved her as any devoted son should, mayhap 'twas all worth it. But still...

She jumped from her chair at the sudden knock at the wooden portal. She had barely muttered her call for the person to enter when the door was thrust open. Killian stood there, his mantle covered in snow while Isabel cowered behind him with a worried frown.

"I tried to tell him he should wait in your hall, my lady, but he refused to listen," she said as she moved in front of Killian who gently pushed her behind him yet again.

Ella waved her hand to dismiss her lady. "There is no harm done, Isabel. Killian is welcome here." She watched the man of her musings as he continued to silently stare at her. "You may go and attend to your duties, Isabel."

Isabel tried to move around him but Killian refused to budge. "If you are certain, my lady." Concerned etched itself across her brow but again, Ella dismissed her with a nod.

The door closed quietly leaving a deafening silence between

the pair with the exception of the crackling fire. Ella went to a nearby table to pour Killian a chalice of wine. She pointed to the chair nearest the fire.

"Come sit and warm yourself. You must be freezing," she murmured, carefully watching his every move. 'Twas the first time in years they were alone together in the same room and her heart raced within her chest.

"The storm is fierce," he replied as he swung his sodden cape off his shoulders and laid it upon a table. He came to the hearth and took the cup from her outstretched hands, their fingers briefly touching sending a shockwave through Ella's body.

"I am glad you survived Berwyck's siege. Conrad said there were many casualties."

"Aye. There is much tae tell of the happenings back home."

Ella nodded. "We expected you sooner."

"I came as soon as I was given permission tae leave," he muttered into his cup before setting the chalice down. He stretched out his hands towards the warmth of the fire. "Where are yer sons? Yer maid said they were not in residence."

Ella sat back down in her chair and Killian took the opposite seat to stare at her as though he could read her very thoughts. She bit back the words she longed to confess to Killian about how Conrad was *their* son. "They were summoned to London to await the king's pleasure. How are your people?"

"The Devil's Dragon has assumed control over Berwyck. The castle and its people are under England's rule once more," he said, while still pondering her most curiously. "But ye knew that, did ye not?

A startled gasp escaped her and she tore her eyes from his to watch the flames of the fire instead. "I have no idea what you are talking about."

A sound came from his lips. Part laugh, part grunt of disbelief. "Ye know of what I speak, woman."

Her eyes narrowed at the way he said *woman*. They had had this conversation many times in their past... or future. "Be careful what you say next, Killian."

His laughter filled her solar. "What could ye possibly do that fate has not already played with its cruel game upon us?"

Her eyes widened. "You know?"

"If my dreams that feel more like memories are true, then aye... I remember ye, Ella. I remember everything about our time together in some insane crazy futuristic way. Tae be honest, it dinnae seem like 'tis possible, so maybe ye can fill in what has been causing me much grief these many years."

Visions of how Faramond reacted when she told him she was from the future quickly flashed through her mind. As much as she wished to confide in Killian, she knew 'twas too soon for him to accept such an admission. 'Til the year that Katherine traveled through time and reached Berwyck's gates, Ella could in no way let him know that such a phenomenon was possible.

"I cannot," she said with a heavy sigh.

"Why?" he growled out.

"'Tis not time."

"What has time got tae do with anything?" he asked reaching for her hand.

Her heart leapt as his calloused fingers smoothed their way across her skin. "*Time* has everything to do with it, although I know that makes no sense to you. Please be patient, Killian. All will work out in due course as it should."

He raised her hand to his lips. "But we loved one another..." he murmured, his voice husky in a tone Ella remembered only too well.

"Aye." 'Twas a simple statement, for she could not manage more than a single word. She did not trust herself to reveal her feelings. Her love for this man before her was never stronger than at this very moment.

"...and love each other still." Killian continued as he all but admitted his love for her.

Her heart cracked wide open even as a sob leaked past her lips at his declaration. How could it not? She had never stopped loving Killian even after he pushed her through the Time gate in order to change her son's destiny.

"Aye," she murmured, while tears rushed to her eyes.

She watched the sense of relief wash across his features. Unprepared when he pulled her towards him, she fell into his lap even as her arm automatically snaked around his neck.

Before she could say that they needed only be patient 'til they could be together, his mouth swooped down upon hers to steal her kiss and she was lost. This was *her* Killian and for once she would not think about the repercussions this moment might cost her.

She pressed herself into his body while his arms tightened around her. His mouth ravished hers and she did not care. Killian was at long last in her arms and her only thought was to rip the clothes from his body so they could make love in her bed.

She tore his lips from his, their breathing ragged as they stared one to the other like the long-lost lovers they were. "Not here," she murmured before placing a quick kiss upon his lips. She stood, and taking his hand she opened her solar door to peer down the passageway. Seeing the way was clear, she led him to her bedchamber and once inside bolted the door. Her back rested against the frame as though she could quickly escape if she chose to do so.

Killian came to her and pressed himself intimately against her. Taking her arms, he lifted them above her head and her breath hitched when he held them with one hand while the other began moving down the side of her body.

"Ye have bewitched me, Ella," he murmured as he began nibbling at her neck.

"How so?" she asked in a breathy tone.

"Because I have dreamed of loving ye for so long I thought I might go mad from waiting tae have ye."

"Then wait no longer, Killian. Love me as I have loved you for as long as I can remember."

"Ella, my love," he whispered, before his lips came crashing down upon hers once more.

Frantic to feel his skin next to her own, her hands tore at his tunic even while he rushed to remove the belt holding his scabbard. The clang of his weapon falling upon the stone floor beneath her feet echoed in the room and when she helped pull his garment over his head, her fingers spread their way across his lightly furred chest. She had waited so long to touch him again and now that this moment was upon them, she was suddenly afraid of what their future might hold.

Killian was still just as perfect as she remember, mayhap even more so since he was currently younger than the last time they had made love upon the forest floor. She lightly traced his broad shoulders, the bulging biceps of his arms, the ridged lines of the muscles of his stomach. She pressed a kiss on his chest and heard his low moan.

Killian gave her no further time to ponder what their coupling might mean to their future. Instead, the remainder of their clothing quickly joined his tunic 'til they fell naked upon her bed. Frantic for him to once more possess her, she urged him to take her without haste. Her body shook when he entered her and before long Ella screamed out his name as she reached her climax. And when Killian followed close behind her and filled her with his seed, Ella knew she was as close to heaven as she would ever get while still walking the face of the earth.

And in that moment when Killian held her close as their breathing returned to normal and he vowed the next time would be more at their leisure, Ella knew she must tell him of their son. She could not allow Killian to return to Berwyck without knowing the truth. She prayed he would understand.

CHAPTER 35

Killian watched the woman across the table as they broke their fast. Last eve had been incredible and he could not remember a time when he had so much enjoyed waking up next to a woman. 'Twas because he loved her with every fiber of his being. Yet, something was off with the fair Lady Ella. She appeared nervous as a newborn colt and every noise made her look like she was about to flee the castle for parts unknown. He reached for her hand and he cradled the shaking limb between both of his hands.

"Ye may as well tell me what is troubling ye this morn, my lady," Killian said in what he hoped was a soothing tone.

"I know not how to begin without revealing too much, too soon," she replied, her voice low as her eyes darted about the room to ensure their conversation remained private. "I already pray that, by our actions last night, we have not somehow ruined our future life together."

He gave a small chuckle. "Ye speak of things that ye have no control over, my love. No one can change their future."

A sound came out of his lady that was more like a sob than a laugh. "You are so very wrong in that assumption, Killian."

He pondered her for a moment before raising her hand to his lips. "Then tell me what ye can. I have already surmised that we loved one another, although how that is possible I cannae fathom. What harm can be done by telling me the rest of whatever is troubling you?"

Her mouth opened and closed several times before she gave a heavy sigh and pulled her hand from his. Reaching for her cup, she took a drink before she answered him. "I have pondered what I can or should reveal and yet the repercussions of me revealing anything to you might cost us all. Mayhap 'tis best if I wait. Everything will fall into place soon enough."

"I cannae force ye to tell me anything ye are uncomfortable with nor shall I press the issue. So let us instead talk about ye moving tae Berwyck so we can wed," he said giving her a bright smile of what he hoped looked like encouragement.

"Wed?" she gasped out. "We cannot wed as yet. There is still much that I must do before we can be together."

He brow furrowed at her words. What game was she now playing? "What do ye mean we cannae wed? After last night, why would ye deny me as yer husband?"

"'Tis not that I would not be honored to be your wife, Killian. I have dreamed of you as my husband for many a year. But you must understand that more time must pass 'til we can have such an outcome."

"And what of last night?" he growled out, frustrated Ella would not see his reasoning. Of course, they must wed.

"What about it?"

"Have ye given no thought that even now there is the possibility that ye may be carrying my bairn within ye?"

Killian watched Ella reach for her stomach and a piece of his heart melted for this woman who might become the mother of his bairn. True, they were older than most couples who would start their lives together, yet they were not too old to still make a child.

"A child," she whispered, "would change our future. What have we done?"

Killian stood and went around the table and sat next to his lady. "We have done nothing wrong, Ella. But if a bairn has been conceived then we must wed. We cannae have our bairn born a bastard and damned in the eyes of God."

"You cannot seriously believe that our child would be damned."

"Ye know how the Church views these things. Would ye condemn our bairn tae such a fate?"

She shook her head. "Nay. I would not wish such an outcome for any child, especially ours."

Ella appeared nervous again and he took her hand once more. "Then wed me, my dearest Ella," Killian whispered as he kissed her knuckles. "Ye would honor me by becoming my wife."

She lowered her head and Killian held his breath while he awaited her words.

"I am sorry, Killian. I love you but I cannot marry you as yet when there are still things that I must do in order for future events to come about. 'Tis of grave import and affects the lives of several people so that they, too, can be happy. I cannot deny them their happiness even if 'tis at the cost of my own."

"I thought ye cared for me!" His raised voice trembled with disappointment.

"I do care for you, Killian. You just need to be patient!"

"Ack! Just how much longer are we tae wait 'til we can be together? Days? Months?" He watched her carefully and her tear-filled eyes told him more than her words ever could. "Years?"

"Aye. Years," she whispered before a sob tore from her lips. "I am sorry, Killian. I love you with every breath I take but you must try to understand…"

"I understand nothing!" he fumed. "Ye tell me ye love me and that we have loved before and yet ye refuse tae become my wife. If this is love, then I want no part of it." He stood to stare at the woman who had crushed his last chance at having a family and the love of a good woman.

"You do not mean that," she cried out with outstretched hands.

"Aye, I do. I care for ye, woman, but ye must think I am a saint if ye think I can wait years before I can claim ye as my bride."

"Are we not worth waiting for? Worth fighting for?" she pleaded.

Killian hesitated before answering. He was hurt and not thinking rationally but still his words tumbled from his mouth. "I leave for Berwyck. If ye find ye are pregnant, send word tae me. We will wed tae give the bairn my name. 'Twill then be up tae ye if ye wish tae openly declare we are husband and wife."

He took one last look upon the woman who had broken his heart before turning to leave her hall. He did not look back even while she yelled out his name.

Returning to Berwyck, he threw himself into training the

clansmen and Conrad to be the fiercest of warriors. When no word came from Ella, he knew any chances of fathering a bairn were at an end. Still… the woman consumed his every waking hour and continued to fill his dreams.

Patience. She had asked him to be patient and he could do little else, for Ella left him no further options. He had little faith left to believe they would ever be together and Killian hardened his heart, knowing he would never love again.

CHAPTER 36

Berwyck Castle
The Year of Our Lord's Grace 1179

Four years! Ella could hardly have imagined another four years would pass before she saw Killian again. But 'twas of her own making, even though she knew in her heart her actions were for the greater good. But she could never erase the look of raw pain in Killian's features when he had last left her that day.

Regret consumed her. After they had made love at Hull, she had sworn she would tell Killian that Conrad was his child and yet fear had frozen the words upon her lips. What if he did not believe her? What if he claimed she was a witch, because what else would a twelfth-century man think about the possibility of a modern-day woman traveling through time? She had changed Faramond's fate once and to have her son become the man she had always hoped he would be was worth the challenges of falling through another Time gate. But she was uncertain if she could duplicate her fate again if Killian denounced her. 'Twas best to let the matter rest. She must only wait three more years before all would fall into place.

'Twas an odd feeling to be sitting in Berwyck's hall with Katherine de Deveraux dining at the other end of the raised dais. Aye, she had saved Katherine once again from the flowing Coquet River near Warkworth Castle and they had traveled the distance to the safety of Berwyck's gates. Eluding the villains who were bent on seeing the lady dead had been no easy task but Ella knew how to survive in the wild, not that there had been a need this second time around. Ella was still astounded as she remembered waking up one morn in the safety of her chamber at Hull with the premonition that she must travel to Warkworth and the hidden hermitage. She had wasted little time leaving the castle in order to make it there in time to save the lady who had become like a daughter to Ella.

Katherine was safe, along with her unborn child. Once winter was upon them, Katherine's husband Riorden would eventually reunite with the wife he currently thought was dead. Ella watched Sir Fletcher, Berwyck's captain of the guard, through lowered lashes and shook her head. Nay… she would not interfere with what Ella knew would not come about regarding the knight's feelings for his friend's wife. Fletcher was destined for another and Ella only needed to wait to have her conversation with Jenna Sinclair, another lady from the future, 'til Ella could finally tell Killian all. Three more years would feel like another lifetime…

A feeling of being watched overcame her and Ella raised her eyes to look about the hall. Killian's blue-green eyes flashed with a burning intensity that Ella could not mistake for anything else but desire. Her heart rejoiced that, despite his last words to her, Killian obviously still felt something for her. But God help her, would he, and Conrad for that matter, ever forgive her for keeping the secret of her son's true sire? To lose the love of not only her son but Killian as well had become her greatest fear. But had she not sacrificed enough during her second quest to find love? She had all but given Conrad to Killian to raise at Berwyck. Ella was grateful to Killian for fostering him even though the man had no idea he was in truth raising his own son.

She shook her head, disrupting her agonizing musings. Killian continued to observe her 'til he gave a nod to his head. 'Twas a silent command to follow when he made his way toward the turret stairs and Ella was left with little doubt that, if she did not do so, the ornery Scot would most likely come back and carry her from the hall over his shoulder like some marauding pirate capturing his prey.

Ella excused herself from the table and made her way up the winding stone stairs. Reaching the third floor where her chamber was located, she made her way down the passageway 'til she reached the alcove she and Killian would sit in, in a different time, when Faramond arrived looking for her. He waited there for her and held out his hand for her to take. Without hesitation, she grasped hold. He pulled her down into his lap. A sense of *déjà vu* swept across her soul causing Ella to shiver. She could only ponder what this conversation with Killian would bring.

"Ella," he murmured, while his hand gently guided her head down so she could receive his kiss.

Lost… she became so lost that all rational thinking once more fled as Killian held her close in his embrace. Oh, how she loved this man! The man who, for all these years, had been waiting for her alone while he sacrificed any happiness he might find with another. She clung to him as though she were starving and only he could satisfy the hunger that flamed in her soul. He deepened their kiss and she moaned as desire swept through her body.

He quickly pulled his lips away, their breathing ragged as they attempted to find air to fill their lungs. She swallowed hard while she waited for what she knew was coming. He would not like her answer.

"Tell me we can be together now that Katherine de Deveraux has returned tae Berwyck," he murmured. He ran his thumb over her cheek in a gentle caress. "She is the reason why ye couldnae say anything to me? This odd business about her and her friends traveling from another place in time?"

"You believe her? You know her story?" she asked in a breathy whisper of awe.

"Amiria and Dristan believe her so I cannae gainsay them. They have told me they saw the proof of the tale with their own eyes when the Lady Katherine and her companions were here months ago. But I must admit I find the whole story tae be some kind of jest tae amuse us, like the traveling bards who come tae our gates. No one can travel through time." He chuckled even while he pulled her closer.

She took his cheeks in her hands. "Aye," she said taking a deep breath before she continued. "They can."

A puzzled frown crossed his brow and Ella reached up to smooth the worry from his face. "Ye cannae possibly be telling me that ye..."

His words trailed off and, before Ella could answer, a servant came down the passageway carrying linens for one of the bedchambers. She quickly stood and turned to peer out the window 'til the woman entered one of the rooms.

"We cannot talk of this in the corridor of Berwyck for any and all to hear my words. But, aye, 'tis true." Taking Killian's hand, they made their way to her chamber where Ella bolted the door.

"I need a drink," Killian declared running his hand through his hair.

Ella went to the table near the fire and poured wine into a cup. Handing it to him, she sat and motioned to the vacant chair next to her. Another sense of *déjà vu* passed over her as she remembered a similar situation at Hull. Oh, how she longed for a day when she and Killian could have new memories of time they shared together. He took a drink of the wine and stared into the chalice as though it held the answers he stood in need of. He finally raised his tortured eyes to stare at her and Ella could see and understand his confusion. 'Twas a lot to take in for a medieval man.

"Did ye know that many years ago Shona, Berwyck's healer and Kenna's mother, told me of ye?"

A gasp escaped Ella. "She knew of me?"

A small smile lit Killian's face. "She dinnae mention ye specifically, only that there would be but one woman who was destined for me. Much like ye, she told me I must have patience before we could be together. Of course, I was full of myself in my youth and couldnae believe such rot when there were plenty of women to choose from tae become my wife once I was ready to wed."

Ella's heart lurched within her chest at the thought of how she might have lost Killian to another in her journey to righting the wrong she had caused her son. Killian had also paid the price for a chance to love someone from his own time. Surely, he must have known all this when he pushed her through the Time gate to alter Faramond's destiny. He had to have known the risk that all might be lost. Yet, sitting across from Killian now showed her that he had no inkling that he had done such an action in their past life.

"I have confirmed your dreams are but glimpses of our past life together," Ella began, only to clamp her lips closed. Afraid she would reveal too much, her doubts began to once more consume her.

"Do ye not mean our future?" he asked rubbing his hand through his beard.

"Aye… I suppose I do," Ella murmured.

"I do not profess tae know all there is about this traveling through Time business, only that such a miracle has brought ye into my life, dear Ella." He gave her a smile but Ella could see 'twas riddled with doubt that she spoke the truth.

"*Time*… both my friend and enemy for many a year now," Ella said before taking a sip of her wine. "I still cannot reveal all to you, Killian, as much as I wish to put your worries to ease."

"I cannae see 'twill make much of a difference. What could Time do tae us that it has not already accomplished by keeping us apart for all our lives? We are together now and 'tis all that matters."

Ella gave a weary sigh knowing the storm that was about to erupt in this chamber once she once more spoke. "I must return to Hull."

"By *Saint Michael's Wings!*" he swore. "What the bloody hell are ye talking about, woman?" His knuckles turned white from clenching the goblet that Ella thought he might snap the stem in two.

She understood his anger but nothing prepared her for when he stood and grabbed her from her chair. He crushed her in a fierce embrace before he tilted her chin so she had no choice but to stare into his furious blue-green eyes.

"Killian, please try to understand..."

"Understand?" he roared. "I understand nothing of what has been going on with our lives all these years. Ye say ye love me and that we were together before, that ye have had tasks that needed to be accomplished before we can be together. Yet ye still deny us a life together! I have lived my life as a bloody Saint waiting for ye and ye still tell me I must needs wait more! Ye ask much of me, Ella."

"I know, but in three more years I will have done all I can to—"

"Ye ask for another three years?" he bellowed before he pushed her away and began to pace the room.

"'Tis a lot to ask, I know," she said quietly, unsure what words might offer Killian the solace he stood in need of.

He stopped his pacing to stare upon her, a frown marring his brow. "I have never loved another," he confessed. "From the first moment ye and yer husband came tae bring yer sons tae Berwyck tae foster I have felt drawn tae ye... a sin, I know, tae covet another man's wife but I cannae unwind the past and my feelings for ye. At least ye were able to have a family while I have had none."

She went to him, placing her hand upon his arm. "You have me. Is it not enough that I love you?"

"If I cannae claim ye as my wife, then ye do not belong to me, Ella."

"What is three more years compared to all we have been through? Certainly 'tis but one small moment etched in time and worth the sacrifice so we can finally be together."

A knock sounded at the door halting his reply.

"Mother. 'Tis Conrad. I was told you were here."

Killian went to the door and slid the bolt open. Conrad's surprised looked startled Ella, especially seeing the two men standing side by side. Everyone must be blind not to see the connection.

"Killian? I was unaware you were having speech with my mother," Conrad said looking between the two of them.

A grunt left Killian's lips. "We are finished," he said before giving a short bow. "My lady, I wish ye safe travels on yer return journey tae Hull."

Ella watched Killian leave and she all but fell into her chair. Conrad went to her before her pressing her cup into her hand.

"Mother, are you well? What did Killian say to upset you?"

Ella took a sip of her wine, almost choking as the liquid slid down her throat. "'Tis nothing, son. Go bolt the door. I have much to confess to you."

Her son appeared just as puzzled as Killian had been. Although she would not tell Conrad that Killian was his father as yet, 'twas time to at least tell her son where she was from. She only prayed he would somehow understand and not react has Faramond had once done during her other lifetime long ago.

Killian sat in the tavern with a cup of ale in one hand and a pretty wench sitting upon his knee. He would drown out Ella in more ways than one this day and he cared not of the consequences come the morn. Setting down his cup, he pulled the bar maid closer and she squealed in delight. He began nibbling at the wench's neck and he heard her giggle.

"'Tis about time ye came tae pay me a visit, Killian. What

took ye so long?" the woman asked while she took his hand and pressed it to her bosom.

He continued to nuzzle her neck. "What I want of ye dinnae require speech between us."

"As long as ye have the proper coin, then I am all yers. I may like ye but I dinnae give myself fer free."

Her raised brow while she awaited his answer had him reaching for the pouch at his belt. He lifted the leather and the jingle of his monies more than indicated he had enough to spare. "I have plenty for yer time."

"Then let me show ye tae my room," she replied before sliding off his lap and holding out her hand.

Her smile brightened in her invitation while she waited for him to take her fingers and Killian had a moment of hesitation sweep across his mind. He frowned with thoughts of Ella but why should he feel remorse for what he was about to do? 'Twas not as though she had not had a lover in her past. Why should he not be allowed a moment's pleasure in the arms of a willing woman?

The door to the tavern slammed open and the portal filled with several of Berwyck's knights and clansmen. A grunt left Killian's lips as though his chance to find solace in the arms of a stranger had just passed him by. Conrad was the last to enter and, while the knights found an empty table against the back wall, the young man made his way to Killian.

Conrad peered at the woman who continued to wait for Killian. "Leave us," Conrad ordered, "and bring ale."

"Killian?" she asked while disappointment flashed quickly in her eyes.

Killian reached for his pouch and gave her a coin. "For yer troubles," he grumbled.

Conrad took a seat next to Killian and before long the maid returned with a cup she set in front of Conrad. As she was about to leave, Killian reached for her arm carrying the pitcher. "Leave it," he said, before gazing upon the young man next to him. "I have a feeling we shall be needing it."

Conrad downed his drink before reaching to refill his cup. "Aye," he said before looking about the room and lowering his voice. "My mother has told me from whence she came, although I have a feeling in my gut that she omits some of her story. Is this why you were arguing?"

"Do ye not mean *when*?" Killian grunted before he, too, took another drink of his ale.

"Aye... *when*," Conrad muttered with a shake of his head, "although I assumed you knew what I was referring to and 'twas not necessary to say it aloud. I would not wish my mother to be called some witch because someone overhears a conversation we should really be having in private."

Killian swore beneath his breath. He may be furious with Ella but he certainly did not wish to cause her harm. He had loved her all his life and, despite her stubborn insistence that they still could not be together, his love for her did not change.

"If yer mother had told me years ago of her origins before Katherine de Deveraux first came to Berwyck, I wouldnae believe such fanciful tales."

Conrad's brow rose in disbelief. "I have my doubts, but you believe her then."

"Aye, that I do, lad. Ye are correct in yer assumption there is more to yer mother's tale," Killian grumbled into his cup. "I suppose she shall reveal all in good time, despite my irritation that she keeps her secrets tae herself."

Conrad leaned forward. "You are in love with her."

A snort left Killian's lips. "I have no inkling what ye be speaking about."

Conrad chuckled. "You do not have to try and hide your feelings for my mother from me, Killian."

"When did ye get so damn smart, lad?" Killian asked, appalled that he could be so easily read.

"Lad?" Conrad laughed. "I am hardly a boy of my youth at a score and six. Besides… Do you honestly think the two of you could have hidden your emotions whenever you happen to be together?"

"'Tis not as though we are in each other's company for long," Killian growled out. "Why, I have spent more time apart from her than we have been together."

"And yet I can still see for myself that you care for her."

"Of course, I care for her," Killian said before reaching for his cup once more. "Do ye object that I fancy for her tae become my wife?"

Conrad slapped Killian's shoulder. "Not at all, but what is stopping you from asking her to wed?"

"Yer mother still has another task tae complete before we can be together. Her words, not mine. My patience grows thin where yer mother is concerned."

"Then 'tis a good thing I came to the tavern when I did, before you made the mistake I perceive was about to happen. Let us drink and the two of us can drown our sorrows so we have no regrets come the morrow."

Killian watched as Conrad refilled their cups. The young man raised his cup in a salute and Killian returned the gesture. He had many regrets in his life. Lucky for him he had not forsaken the lady he loved for a meaningless tumble with a woman he would easily forget.

CHAPTER 37

Berwyck Castle
The Year of Our Lords Grace 1182

Ella was weary to the bone while she walked the shoreline near Berwyck Castle. Her shoes dangling from her fingertips, the ocean waves stung her sore feet after traveling miles by foot. Memories flashed across her mind as not one but two lifetimes in twelfth-century England fused together as one. She prayed the sacrifice would all be worth it. Aye. Finally. 'Twas time for the last piece of her commitments to fall into place from her past life. Ella knew within her heart Jenna Sinclair would be in residence at Berwyck. Once Ella and Jenna spoke, then Ella would confess all to Killian and Conrad. Her destiny would at last come to fruition: she and Killian would be together.

As she continued walking, it came as no surprise when she heard the thundering of horses coming from behind her. A smile lit her face when she turned to witness once again the incredible sight of Dristan of Berwyck's army galloping in formation. After all… this had already happened once in her past and this just completed the circle of her life. She would be glad when she could move forward to make new memories from this point forward.

"Ah, Lady Ella," Lord Dristan said with a welcoming smile. "A pleasure to see you once again. I pray you shall be gracing Berwyck's halls for a time? 'Twill please my lady to see you again."

Ella was just about to tell him to drop the *lady* title as she would have urged in her previous life. But her past had been altered and Lord Dristan would now know her as Lady Ella of Hull. Hopefully, little else had changed that might have adverse effects on how her life might proceed.

"It would be my pleasure, my lord, to stay at Berwyck for as long as you will have me," she said in the hope that all would be well.

Dristan leaned forward to rest his arm upon the pommel of his saddle. "Your presence in my hall will indeed please many. Is this not so, Killian?"

Ella acknowledged the older knight next to Dristan's horse with a slight nod for she was unsure how he would greet her after their last parting. He was still just as handsome as he had always been and perchance even more so, for this older version of Killian was the one Ella had fallen in love with.

They had been through so much. Would he reject her now that she could finally tell him all and they could be together? She was momentarily startled by the look he gave her with those mesmerizing blue-green eyes, for 'twas an appreciative one. Thank the heavens… he still cared for her!

"Aye, my laird. 'Tis always our honor to have Lady Ella

residing within Berwyck Castle," Killian declared, while his gaze once again swept her from head to toe.

She felt herself blush, as any young maiden might have done from receiving the admiring glances of a handsome suitor. She must look a fright as she tried to remember how to proceed with the rest of this initial conversation. Those knowing eyes of Killian's continued to hold her own causing her blush to heighten considering the heat rushing to her flushed face.

Dristan's merry chuckle brought her out of her silent musings. "We have left the fair woman speechless, it seems, Killian. Assist the lady so she may ride with you," he ordered.

"'Tis hardly necessary, my lord. Berwyck is close enough and the walk will do me good."

Dristan grimaced when his gaze traveling to her abused feet. "You have walked far enough in your latest pilgrimage, if I were to guess, considering the state you are in. But 'tis of no consequence. I insist you ride with us. We must make haste, for we are in great need of sustenance to fill our bellies and quench our thirst. I refuse to allow a woman in our company to continue her travels without escort. See to her, Killian."

"Aye, my laird," Killian answered, dismounting from his horse as Dristan waved his arm and his men put their steeds into motion.

Yanking on the reins of his mount, Killian moved forward to stand before Ella. Looping the leather straps around the pommel, he offered her his assistance in order to mount the huge animal.

"May I, Lady Ella?" he inquired, holding out his hand to her.

She gave a weary sigh. There was no sense in attempting to remain indifferent to the orders he had been given. "If you must obey your lord, then I suppose I must too. But for heaven's sake, please call me Ella. There is no reason to be so formal."

"'Tis not seemly ye should ask such of me, my lady, especially when others are still near."

Her brow rose at his reference to several knights that hung back to ensure Killian's safe return to the castle. Ella was certain 'twas a precautionary measure for one knight or clansman traveling alone could be prey to villain's bent on doing harm.

"Very well, then. I suppose I must obey," she grumbled.

She took his outstretched hand and was briefly surprised when a tingle raced up her arm. He must have felt is too, because his eyes momentarily widened at their touch. He took her hand and placed it upon his shoulder as he in turn lifted her by her waist to place her upon his horse.

Once she was settled, Killian placed his foot in the stirrup and swung himself into the saddle. Since Ella was placed behind him, she made a fast grab for his waist when he flicked the reins and his horse bolted into motion. Her breath left her with his nearness and she swore she heard him give a chuckle.

"Tell me, Killian," she said quietly. "Is Jenna Sinclair in residence at Berwyck?"

"Is she…" he began before she cut off the rest of his words.

"…aye. She is the last part of the past that must be completed, if you take my meaning."

"Since we have been out on patrol at an outlying village, I cannae know who is at Berwyck, especially if 'tis one of you future women," he said gruffly. "But if she is there, ye must find her so we can at last be together."

She tightened her grip around his waist all the while hoping for the best. 'Twas not 'til Killian was helping her dismount and her body slid down against his own, that his mask of indifference slipped from his features. He continued to hold her, staring down into her eyes.

"We have done this before," he murmured in startled surprise as though all their future memories together flashed inside his mind.

"Aye, Killian," she replied in a hushed tone, for she did not think she could say more when he looked at her in such a manner. She reached up to cup his check and his hand covered hers before giving it a gentle squeeze.

And then he smiled and Ella's heart near burst with joy. Happiness overwhelmed her and she could only pray that all would work out as it should once she told him the rest of their story.

For there was no longer any need to leave Berwyck to search for Henry. She knew whom she loved and had fallen back in time for. He stood before her now with all the love he held for her shining in his magnificent blue-green eyes.

Killian stood against the stones of the passageway waiting for Ella to leave Amiria's solar. He knew the Lady Jenna was inside and his lady was having speech with her. He did not need to be privy to their conversation. He now knew of Ella's origins and he did not care that she was not of his time… or mayhap she was, seeing as she had lived through her twelfth-century life not once but twice. He ran a hand through his hair in frustration that the woman he cared for and who had slipped through time for him was only a short distance away. They had waited their entire lifetime to be together and now their lives could finally begin.

The door finally swung open and, as Ella exited the room, he lessened the distance between them. Taking her hand, he began leading her down the passageway, down the turret to the floor below, and quickly made his way to her bedchamber. As they entered, he slid the bolt to ensure their privacy.

"Killian…" she said in a breathy whisper. "My love, there is much that I still must confess to you before we go any farther."

"Later…" he said as he crossed the room to take her in his arms.

"But 'tis of grave import," she tried again but Killian refused to listen to anything more she might say. He had waited too long to have her once more beneath him.

"Later…" he repeated and he rushed to take off their garments.

Naked, he could only stare in wonder at the beautiful woman who wrapped her arms around his neck. He carried her to her bed for there was no need for any further words between them. He began to love her as he had dreamed of for all his life and when she yelled out his name when she found her release, he was content. They had found one another again and Time no longer was their enemy.

CHAPTER 38

Killian listened to conversations around him with only half an ear. His attention centered around Ella... *his* Ella, although she currently danced with another much to his dismay. He gave a brief chuckle, thinking of when they had made love earlier. He could have no doubts that she still loved him after such a tumbling. But his one desire was to get the woman alone so he could put into place the memories that were scrambled inside his head.

Aye... He seemed to remember everything that had occurred in their past — or was it their future — even though he was having a difficult time dealing with it all. His eyes kept waiting for the keep door to open, for he could almost see Faramond rushing through it, an angry man bent on finding his mother, even though Killian knew this time would be different. There was now no cause for Faramond to be angry for, if Killian's memories were true, he had himself pushed Ella through the Time gate in order to change her son's fate. 'Twas Killian choice alone. He had no one to blame for remaining unwed except himself. He shook his head, knowing all this time he had blamed Ella and her stubbornness to set matters aright when he really should have carried the burden himself. How could he have known?

Flashes of memory raced across his mind. Arguing with the stubborn woman that he would see her to her long-lost love, although 'twas obvious to all that Killian and Ella had feelings for one another. Not that she had admitted such aloud. More visions flashed across his mind: traveling at dawn to take her to Henry de Rune; hiding in the forest so her son would not find them and waking up to the woman curled around his body as though she belonged there; traveling to Warkworth and Ella's abduction from the Hermitage; planning her escape with the help of Ella's servant; and finally professing their love to one another. Mayhap these memories were not as scrambled as he had just thought. They seemed perfectly clear now that he concentrated on them.

Killian's heart skipped a beat, remembering how they had made love on the forest floor, followed by his decision that, in order for them to have a life together, he must allow Ella the chance to change her son's fate. How could he have known that he, too, would have the chance to live his life over again?

As if on cue, the keep door opened and in walked Faramond, who took off his rain drench cape. Handing the garment to a servant, he made his way to his mother who received him with open arms. 'Twas obvious Killian had made the right decision, for there was no longer any animosity in Faramond's demeanor toward the mother who gave him life.

There was only one thing that continued to plague Killian and that was the fact Ella had another son before Faramond was even born. Mayhap he was just confused, for she had never mentioned anything from her past the first time she had traveled to Berwyck. He took a hard look at Conrad while he strode across the hall to envelope his brother in a fierce hug. The two men conversed for several minutes before Conrad rejoined a lady at one of the tables. Killian's eyes narrowed as though looking at the lad for the very first time. By *God's Bones!* What if...

Ulrick gave Killian a shove with his shoulder. "You should go claim the next dance with her, Killian, before another sweeps her away," the knight chuckled, before taking a sip of his ale as laughter from the other men chimed in.

Killian's glance slid to his friend and, whereas before he had denied that he knew what Ulrick had been speaking about, this time he would in no way partake in his banter.

He downed his drink, slamming his goblet down upon the table. "I think I will do just that," he said, before making his way toward the woman he cared for but who had much explaining to do!

Her back was toward him and she jumped when he reached out to touch her elbow. Killian watched as she appeared to attempt to catch her breath.

"Killian," she exclaimed. "You startled me."

He peered down at her and wondered how she might explain herself. "My apologies, my lady. 'Twas not my intent to alarm ye. I only came tae ask for the privilege of the next dance." He held out his hand for her to take.

Her warm fingers touched the palm of his hand and a tingling sensation rushed up his arm. *Bloody hell!* What this woman did to him could not easily be explained. He led her into the middle of the floor to join the other dancers but he could see for himself that she appeared nervous. He could only imagine the reason why.

"What are ye afraid of?" he asked.

She missed a step and tumbled into his chest. He took advantage of her clumsiness and pulled her into his arms even while the remaining dancers blurred by them as they continued onward. He raised her chin so she had no choice but to look upon him.

"I am terrified that once I tell you the rest of my story you will be angry with me. We should have spoken of this before we made love earlier but you near took my breath away. I could in no way deny you when there was nothing more that I wanted than to be in your arms."

"Then let us find a quiet place where we can converse in private so there are no further secrets between us," he said as he began ushering her from the room.

She halted before they reached the turret steps. "Bring Conrad."

"And Faramond?" he asked.

"Nay!"

"Why?" Killian raised a brow seeing how upset Ella was.

Her eyes darted to her son across the room conversing with the laird of Berwyck. "He must never know…"

"As you wish, my lady. I shall go fetch Conrad." That she would wish her son to be privy to her confession practically confirmed what Killian had already surmised. Somehow, someway, Conrad was his son. Killian left her standing near the stairs before he made his way to the young man.

He placed his hand on Conrad's shoulder. "Yer mother wishes to have a private word with us," he said, before Conrad excused himself from the lady he had been conversing with and the two men strode back to Ella.

Killian's heart beat a rapid staccato in his chest as they made their way to Amiria's solar. Seeing the room empty, they entered and Ella quickly went to a nearby table to pour them all a chalice of wine. Once she offered them their cups, she went to stand near the fire before she motioned for them to take a seat.

Conrad was the first to break the silence among them. "What is this all about, mother?" he asked before setting his cup down and leaning his arms upon his legs.

Killian took a gulp of his wine before he, too, set his chalice down upon the table. "I believe yer mother is about tae tell us the rest of her story. Is this not so, Ella?"

"Aye and I will first offer my apologies for not being able to tell you sooner, but I believed there to be much at stake."

Conrad turned to peer at Killian who only shrugged and waited for Ella to continue. Only God above knew how her son would react to what he would learn this day. Killian prayed he would also be calm enough to accept whatever Ella would at last reveal.

Ella paced before the hearth, knowing this conversation would either break her connection to the two men who sat before her or would only strengthen their relationship.

"You both know that I am not originally from this time. I have already told you both how or when I fell through Time on the first occasion and... well... also a second time where I found that I was a younger version of myself. I was given the chance to live a life in the twelfth-century and in order to accomplish this, there were certain sacrifices I had to make in order to be reunited with the one person I loved. I married and had... a child," Ella hesitated to look at her son.

Conrad smiled at her but when she shook her head, his grin faded. "What are you not saying, mother?"

She took a deep breath before she continued. "I had a child... Faramond... but when my husband died and I told Faramond I was from the future, he called me a witch, casting me out from Hull and forbidding me from ever coming back again."

"I do not understand. My brother is two years younger than I am," Conrad said before Killian interrupted.

"Let her finish," he said and nodded for Ella to continue. Ella stared upon Killian who appeared so calm. Would he remain so or would his Scottish temper put an end to whatever love he had held for her all these years? Ella only knew she was nervous and scared, feeling as though she was about to jump out of her skin.

"I traveled from town to town never staying in one place for long, especially when I learned Faramond was searching for me. Apparently, he had fallen out of favor with the king and needed me to return to Hull in order to save his estate. Terrified, I learned to live off the land and 'twas not 'til I saved Katherine de Deveraux from a river and we made our way to Berwyck did I feel that mayhap I would one day be free of my own son and his ambitions for wealth and fame."

"This hardly sounds like my brother. Where do I fit in with this whole far-fetched tale?" Conrad grumbled, his brow crossed in confusion as he took another drink of his wine.

"'Twas not until I had spoken with Jenna Sinclair that I had realized that 'twas time to meet the man I thought I had originally fallen through time for, Henry de Rune. Killian volunteered to take me to him."

A grunt left Killian. "Volunteered? I seem tae remember 'twas more like I felt obligated tae see ye tae safety so ye dinnae travel alone, even if ye knew 'twas wrong."

"I knew no such thing at the time, you stubborn Scot," Ella retaliated. "If you recall back then, I thought I was still in love with Henry."

Killian grunted before reaching for his chalice. "If ye had only opened yer heart then we wouldnae have had tae travel anywhere and could have stayed here at Berwyck and wed!"

"You of all people should know that I had to complete what I thought was my path to finding love!" she bellowed. "You also know that I did find it but with *you*!"

"Aye. I know that now and as of just a few moments ago, I assumed the rest," Killian said with a quick glance at Conrad.

Ella stumbled back against the table, the pitcher of wine dangerously close to toppling over before she caught it. "You *know...*" she whispered.

Killian rubbed the back of his neck but never took his eyes from his lady. "Ye kept yer secret well, even from me," he muttered with a frown. "But aye... As I just said, I guessed."

Conrad stood and began to pace the room. "If I could interrupt this lovers spat—

"Conrad!" Ella gasped out.

Conrad held up his hand. "Mother, please... 'Tis not as though I have not known that the two of you," he waved his hand between them, "have been *not* having some love affair for some time now. I am not blind nor am I a child any longer. 'Tis your sin, and it is you who must seek forgiveness with God."

"Ye will not dishonor yer mother, Conrad," Killian warned,

pointing his finger towards the young man. "There is still more for her tae tell ye."

Conrad gave a heavy sigh. "That is where I am confused. You are both talking about the Lady Jenna as though this was in the past when I know she has not long arrived at Berwyck. This whole traveling through Time business is almost too much to believe."

Ella watched when Killian stood and went to Conrad, placing his hand upon his shoulder. "Aye... yer mother speaks of the past and this is true. I have seen the proof myself, lad, when Lady Katherine first arrived. Her presence at Berwyck seems tae have linked this place tae those in another time who are searching for love. In yer mother's case, I can only assume she was destined to save Lady Katherine and eventually make her way here."

Conrad went back to his seat, his hand shaking when he reached for his wine. "You still have not told me what I am missing here."

Ella went to take a small stool, placed it before her son and took his hands. "Conrad... you know I love you with all my heart," she began.

"Of course, mother, as I love you," he said with a small smile.

"Then let me finish my story."

"Does it have one of those happily ever after endings you used to tell me about in my youth?" Conrad asked while he fidgeted in his chair.

Ella leaned forward to kiss his cheek. "I can only hope so."

"Then proceed."

Ella's stare momentarily rested on Killian and her heart leapt inside her chest while she saw all the love he held for her shining in his magnificent yes.

"Tell him, Ella."

She drew a heavy breath. "When Faramond came to Berwyck in search of me in our past, Killian agreed to take me to find the place where I would stumble into Henry upon the road. But things changed while we were traveling. I began to realize that I had not fallen through Time to meet Henry but to fall in love with Killian. He had always been kind to me whenever I traveled to Berwyck and we were friends. While we traveled, we declared our feelings for one another and made love.

"But I was tormented that Faramond had become this horrible person. Killian understood what I was going through and, if I remember correctly, I said something about wishing I could change my past in order to save my son. I was wishing I had never told Faramond I was from the future because he could not fathom such an occurrence and believed 'twas sorcery when I claimed 'twas true."

Killian went to Ella, placing his hands upon her shoulder. "I came tae the conclusion that we could never have a life together when yer mother was so upset with Faramond and the man he had become. So… when we heard de Rune's horse coming closer upon the road, we saw the Time gate open and I pushed yer mother through it so she could change her son's future."

Conrad placed his head in his hands. "I still do not understand where I fit in to this insane conversation."

Ella took a deep breath. "The past blurred together with what was now my present. The difference was that, only now, I knew my purpose had grown larger than our original plan. I had to have my situation play out with Henry as it did in my past life so I could fall through time... again... to marry Simon and save my son by not telling him where I came from. But more importantly, before I could have a child with Simon, I needed to ensure the babe I unknowingly carried from my future life was safe. The child I had conceived with Killian. That child was you, Conrad. Killian is your father."

Ella watched the emotions wash across her son's face and she waited for his anger to erupt.

"What the bloody hell!" Conrad bellowed yanking his hands roughly from Ella's grasp. He turned his hostile eyes to Killian. "How long have you known?"

Killian gave a heavy sigh. "As I said, I only just surmised the fact a short while ago this eve. Since yer mother's arrival earlier today, my memories have all returned tae recall our previous time together."

Conrad turned hostile eyes toward Ella and her heart cracked to see what she had done to her beloved son.

"How could you make me believe that my father was dead all these years? That Lord Simon cared for me?" Conrad asked, his voice shaking with anger.

"Lord Simon did care for you as much as he cared for Faramond. No man was ever prouder," Ella said twisting her hands together.

"And what of Killian? How could you have taken this knowledge away from him all these years and me as well?"

"'Twas my greatest fear someone would put the pieces together that you were father and son. I had to conceal Killian was your father but, in every sense of the word, he has raised you to become the man you are today. If you look to your heart you will realize that, since you fostered with him, Killian has spent more time with you than I ever was allowed."

"You stole from us the fact that my father was very much alive!" Conrad bellowed.

"And in a round about way, I sacrificed my own time with you in order for you to foster at Berwyck where I knew Killian resided." Tears formed in her son's eyes and Ella wished she could erase the pain she had caused. But what else could she do? Did she just trade one son's destiny for another?

Conrad wiped his eyes. "I will never forgive you," he growled. "Go back to Hull, mother. You have no place here at Berwyck."

A sob tore from Ella's lips as she watched her son begin to leave the chamber. "Conrad," she cried out, but he refused acknowledge her, slid the bolt on the door once he reached it, and left without a backwards glance.

"Oh, Killian! What have I done to you both," she sobbed, before he lifted her from the stool and wrapped her in his arms. She clung to his strength, for he did not seem to be as upset with her as she thought he would be.

"All will be well, Ella. Ye just need tae give him some time tae calm down and accept the truth," Killian said, caressing her hair.

"You must find him. Mayhap he will listen to you," Ella said lifting her head from his chest to gaze upon at him. "Please tell me you will go look for him."

"Ye know I will, but I must know ye are going to be alright before I leave ye."

"Aye, but I cannot stay here. I will return to Hull to give Conrad time to a come to terms that you are his father."

A snort left Killian. "Ye will do no such thing. Yer place is here with us, not at Hull."

"I will not take Berwyck from my son. This is his home and I will not make this harder on him by staying where I am not wanted."

"Ye stubborn woman. Ye are wanted here by me!"

"But Conrad…"

"…will learn to deal with the situation with time. And we have all the time in the world, Ella, to now be together as a family."

"You forgive me for keeping my secret?" she asked in a breathy whisper, while praying Killian would not hold this against her.

"I will admit I was confused and a bit angry when all my memories came storming inside my head today and I realized the truth of it. But there is nothing tae forgive, Ella. We have traveled through Time. Mayhap 'twas not done together but our lives were still intertwined and ye have given me a son. I cannae ask more from ye than that," he said with a smile before kissing her forehead, "with the exception of finally becoming my wife."

Air rushed from Ella's lungs as she realized she had not lost Killian even though he did not understand her desire to leave Hull to give Conrad the time he needed without her interference. She pulled on his tunic and stood on the tips of her toes to give him a quick kiss.

"Go find our son," she said and heard Killian's chuckle. His smile lit a fire in her heart.

"I like the sound of that."

"Go on with you then."

"As my lady commands," Killian said with a bow before he left the room.

Ella took several moments to compose herself and soon followed, making her way down the turret steps and out of the keep. She thought to find Kenna, Berwyck's healer, in order to find out if there was anything else Ella needed to fear. But when she heard the raised voices of Conrad and Killian on the far end of the inner bailey, any further thoughts of staying at Berwyck fled. She needed to return to Hull. She would not anger Conrad any more than she already had. She could only pray that Killian would understand.

CHAPTER 39

Killian grabbed hold of Conrad's arm and began ushering him towards the chapel. "Ye will keep yer voice down 'til we have a closed door between us and the rest of Berwyck," he muttered, growing a bit impatient with the angry man next to him. "There is no need for everyone tae hear our family business."

"*Family,*" Conrad scoffed. "What the hell is family? A closed door will in no way keep out and erase the hurt racing through me from what my own mother has kept from me!"

"Ye have a right tae be hurt, Conrad, but if ye slow down tae think on the matter, ye would come tae realize yer mother had no choice," Killian said. Opening the chapel door, his eyes peered into the darkened interior to ensure they were alone.

"Why are you not angry with her?" Conrad hissed before skimming his fingers through his hair. "She took years from us."

"Did she?" he asked quietly. Killian stared at the younger version of himself. How blind had he been not to see the resemblance? How could he have ever surmised that Ella had gotten pregnant from their first time together so many years ago? Especially since he had no memory of it.

Conrad stopped his pacing. "Well... of course she did."

"I dinnae see how. Yer mother was right in many instances," Killian held up his hand to halt his son's words, "wrong, too, but right on most accounts. Ye have been with me far longer than she was ever given the chance to be. I had the better chance tae know the man ye have become, with the exception of yer rare visits tae Hull. Ye have made a home here at Berwyck. Ye are considered one of its people and would defend this place 'til yer last dying breath just as any of us who have pledged their allegiance tae its laird."

Conrad went to sit on one of the benches before resting his head in his hands. "I feel as though I have lost everything that I have known to be the truth of my life," he whispered.

Killian went to sit next to him, placing his hand upon his shoulder. "Ye have lost nothing, son, but have gained a father who loves ye."

"My *father*," he said softly. Conrad lifted his head and Killian saw the disbelief flash quickly across his visage. "I can hardly fathom I have a father who lives."

"Aye, although ye know I have thought of ye as the son I never had for many a year now. If ye recall, I even said such tae ye during the siege of Berwyck when I ordered ye tae see tae Aiden's safety and then get yerself tae Hull."

Conrad raised his head to stare at Killian. "I remember, but still..."

"'Twill be an adjustment for all of us, yer mother included. She has suffered the most out of everyone."

"How so?"

"Can ye imagine the burden she must have carried for all her life, not once but twice? Many lives depended on her following the path she trod. Tae be honest, I am not sure I would have been up tae such a monumental task, but she accomplished everything she set out tae do. I believe we are lucky tae know such a woman, who has devoted her life tae ensure the happiness of others even at the cost of her own well-being."

"Traveling through Time…" Conrad said in awe. "Who would have thought such a feat was even possible."

Killian lowered his voice. "We have known for some years that 'twas happening around England and, now with Lady Jenna's appearance, just down below on our very own beach. But we must keep this secret tae ourselves, Conrad. Many lives depend upon it. We do not wish harm tae come tae those we have come to care for, especially yer mother. I am certain ye know the fate for those who are condemned as a witch."

"But surely my own brother can be told?" Conrad said as though the burden was already a heavy weight to bear.

"Nay! Faramond can never be told. Yer mother did not go through all this for a second time just for history tae possibly repeat itself."

"Has it not already been repeated?" Conrad scoffed with a shake of his head.

Killian chuckled. "Well, ye may have that aright, lad. But there is no need for yer mother tae go in search of the man she thought she had loved in her past lives for he is sitting right here next tae ye."

Conrad peered at him through the darkened chapel. "You really do love her, do you not?"

"I have kept yer mother close tae my heart for many a year and have loved no other but her. Even in our past life, I cared for her but I knew she loved another. But love will find ye no matter ye think it impossible."

"Perchance one day 'twill find me as well," Conrad declared with a small smile before his face fell. "I must find my mother and ask her forgiveness for my hasty words."

"She loves ye, Conrad, just as I do. I am most certain she forgave ye the moment ye left the chamber," Killian said before he stood.

Conrad rose as well and silence filled the space between them before Killian reached forward to embrace his son. With a hearty slap upon his son's back, the two men left the chapel to go in search of Ella.

But 'twas the alarmed look on Amiria's face as she raced across the bailey that gave the men pause in their quest. She rushed to Killian, concern etched across her brow.

"You must go and fetch Ella," she ordered.

Killian took the younger woman's arm with a laugh. "We were just on our way tae yer solar. 'Tis where we left her a short while ago."

Amiria waved her arm towards the stables. "Get to your horse, Killian. Kenna just informed me that Ella was seen leaving Berwyck. If you hurry, you should be able to catch up with her on the beach."

"That stubborn woman," Killian growled out. Turning he hurried toward the stable.

"I will go with you," Conrad said falling into step with Killian.

Killian stopped to look upon the man before bracing his hand on Conrad's shoulder. "Nay. I will bring yer mother back tae Berwyck but I think she and I must have this conversation tae ourselves."

Conrad lifted his hands in defeat with a smirk. "If ye say so… father," he replied quietly. "Bring her back where she belongs."

Killian nodded and hastened his way across the bailey. He would finally make Ella see reason even if it killed them both!

CHAPTER 40

Ella made her way across the beach, the satchel she carried feeling heavy in her hands. Heading south, her only thought was to distance herself from her oldest son in order to give him the time he needed to come to terms with all she had told him. He would eventually see reason, would he not? Otherwise, everything she had done in *this* lifetime would have been for naught. She did not think she had the strength to try to go through the Time gate for a third time. 'Twas a lot to ask of any one woman, especially one who had already lived her life this many times. Ella shook her head. Besides... what if she only made things worse instead of fixing yet another problem that had arisen from her meddling with Time?

A vague memory of her modern-day life flashed across Ella's mind. Changing her past for Faramond's sake had given them an altered present. Had she messed with the fabric of time too much and angered the *Time Faeries*? Would she suddenly be ripped from twelfth-century England to find out only a few seconds had passed in the modern-day world and she would be back in Florida as though none of this had happened? Her hands trembled at the thought of never seeing Killian or her sons again. Surely God, or Time, would not be so cruel. Not when she was so very close to having everything she had ever wanted.

She brushed away the tears of sorrow creeping from her eyes. She had been so close to having it all. She should have known that not everything would go as she had planned it all in her head! 'Twas all her fault for messing with Time in the first place.

The sound of thundering hooves caused her to panic. Looking backwards, her eyes widened to see her Scotsman bearing down on her at an alarming speed while he raced his horse across the beach. As he drew closer, she could see the frown etched across his features. He was furious with her for leaving Berwyck, but surely he could understand why.

Ella quickly jumped out of the way as Killian yanked upon the reins of his horse, bringing the steed to a halt but inches from where she now stood. Leaping from the saddle, he reached out for her and gave her a mighty shake.

"Where the devil do ye think ye are going, woman?" he growled fiercely.

"You know where I am headed, Killian," she exclaimed while attempting to rip her arms free from his grip. "And you should refrain from using that tone with me. You know how I dislike it when you call me *woman* in such a manner!"

"Ye belong with me at Berwyck!"

"I belong at Hull 'til my son comes to terms with what he has learned this day," she retaliated with a stomp of her foot.

"Ye are a foolish woman, Ella," he said with a wistful sigh.

"And you are as stubborn as they get," she replied attempting to hide her smirk. Ella could tell Killian was still upset at her but she could also see his eyes twinkling with delight. She put her arms around his waist.

"Aye that I am. I suppose we shall have many years of arguments in our foreseeable future."

"I can think more enjoyable ways to spend our time together," she whispered.

"Can ye now?" he said with a laugh.

"Aye, that I can," she declared with a soft smile. "You know I love you, Killian, do you not?"

He bent down and kissed her forehead. "As I love ye, Ella."

She laid her head upon his chest. Mayhap all would work out as it should. "But what of Conrad?" She hated to ruin this moment between them but she still worried about her son. 'Twas a mother's lot to always be concerned about their children.

Killian tightened his arms around her. His voice softened before she felt him kiss the top of her head. "Conrad is already asking ye tae forgive him for his hasty words tae ye."

A gasp escaped her lips. "You made him see reason? He understands?"

"As much as anyone can understand this business of traveling through Time. I am as much tae blame for what has happened as ye are. After all, I am the one who pushed ye through the Time gate so ye could alter Faramond's life. If I recall, ye were completely against such a journey."

"'Twas a good decision, although I must admit I hated you for it at the time. But look how everything turned out for the best. Faramond is none the wiser and is a man I can now proudly call my son. And Conrad... Mayhap this, too, was a blessing. I might not have been able to carry our babe to term as my older self, at least back here in twelfth-century England. In modern days, there would have been medical technology to see it through, not that I would wish to have a baby at this age. I am still uncertain how 'twas possible I conceived at all."

"'Twas a miracle, tae be sure and I willnae say I am disappointed. Ye gave me a son, although I have spent my life not knowing he was mine."

"If you but opened your eyes you would have seen he looks exactly like you in your younger days," Ella said giving his chest a gentle nudge with her finger. "I should not have had to tell you he was your son."

"How was I tae know this?" he muttered. "Ye were married and when ye first brought the lads tae foster at Berwyck, ye dinnae even show us yer face. I had no idea of who ye were, let alone any recollection of feelings we may have had for one another in a past life together. Why would I think that Conrad was my son?"

Ella gave a heavy sigh and snuggled into Killian's chest. "We are arguing again. Perchance we can just move forward and make new memories together. 'Twould be a welcoming change instead of trying to ensure the past turns out as it should."

Killian took her chin so she could stare up into those remarkable eyes. "Ye changed Faramond's past, Ella, and brought our son into this world. Ye accomplished everything ye set out tae do and more. 'Tis no wonder why I love such an incredible woman."

Ella blushed at his words. It had been such a long wait to hear such compliments and her heart near burst with joy to listen to Killian's tender words. "I am just glad we can now all be together," she said, before pulling out of his arms. She took a knife she kept hidden in her boot and sliced the hem of her dress. She held out her hand with a smile. "I have something for you."

"Do ye now," he replied with a chuckle.

"Just take it, you stubborn Scot," she murmured opening up her fingers. His gasp of surprise caused Ella to smile.

"Ye still had it all this time?" Disbelief swept across his face as his fingers trembled when he took the silver band. "I thought mayhap ye had lost it long ago since ye did not mention the ring earlier. 'Twas my mother's."

"I had a hunch it had belonged to someone important to you. 'Tis only right I now return it to you."

He took her hand and placed the ring on her finger. "It has always belonged to you, the woman that I love."

"As I love you, Killian."

"Then ye shall marry me."

Her brow quirked upward. "Are you asking me or telling me we shall wed?"

A chuckle rumbled in his chest. "I suppose if I am tae halt another argument between us, then I am asking ye."

"Smart man," she laughed.

"Will ye finally wed with me, my lovely Ella?"

"I thought you would never ask," she whispered.

He brow quirked upward. "And…"

She cupped his cheek, running her thumb over the stubble of his beard. "Aye, I shall take you as my husband, my dearest Killian. Now kiss me to seal our fate."

"I am yers tae command, my lady," Killian said, before leaning down to place his lips upon hers.

'Twas a kiss she had dreamed of filled with the promises of at last being able to claim one another. Two lifetimes she had waited for this man and if she had to do it all over again she would. Killian would always be worth traveling through Time in order for them to be together. Love had truly found them and Ella would always be humbly grateful for her second chance at love.

For Ella was finally content knowing she could now start her life anew. She was where she belonged right here and now at this place in Time. She was finally in Killian's arms and there was no place on earth that she would rather be.

EPILOGUE

Berwyck Castle
Two se'nnights later

Killian proudly watched his beautiful wife as she danced to a lively tune in Berwyck's great hall. His belly full after their wedding feast and a mug of ale near at hand made him most content. Aye... he may have had to wait another lifetime to be with the woman he loved but 'twas worth such a sacrifice.

He chuckled in remembrance when he told Father Donovan in no uncertain terms that he would marry the lovely Lady Ella without delay. His lady had something to say on the matter, however, when she insisted she needed time to prepare a proper gown. They had argued, which was hardly unusual, but in the end, he let Ella have her way. What was a couple more se'nnights compared to the rest of their lives?

Amiria linked her arm through his while sitting next to him.

"Are you happy, Uncle?" she asked before turning to carefully watch him. The color of her violet eyes continued to amaze him no matter how old he got.

Her term of endearment for him had always touched his heart. Aye, he and her father had been more than just friends. Killian had watched over Amiria and her siblings for all of their lives. He was proud to claim this young woman as family and, naturally, as part of the MacLaren clan no matter that she was now wed with bairns of her own.

"Aye, of course I am. Ella and I are at last wed. How could I not be happy?" he declared with a bright smile, but it fell when he observed Amiria's puzzled look. "Whatever is the matter, lassie? Are ye and Dristan having problems?"

"Nay, of course not. I love him today as much as I did when we first wed." She gave a troubled sigh before continuing. "I guess I somehow always assumed my brothers and sisters would live here at Berwyck, although that is a fanciful thought, is it not? Naturally they would wed or go on about their lives in other places."

"Sabina is here," Killian said nodding in the young woman's direction as she sat in a chair near the hearth. Dristan stood close at hand as though guarding her. But 'twas not hard to notice Amiria's twin Aiden was missing, as were Lynet and Patrick.

Amiria rested her head on his arm as she did when she a small bairn. "I know you and Ella told Dristan and me privately what happened with her traveling through Time again, but somehow I hoped such a miracle might mayhap…" Her words trailed off yet Killian knew what she was asking without saying the words.

"Ye are speaking of yer parents." Killian voice was low. If only…

"Aye."

"Apparently there are some things Time cannae change, lass, and death is one of them. Yer parents loved one another as much as any two souls can. Yer mother died bringing life tae Patrick and yer father mourned her loss 'til he at last joined her after the siege. If I could have changed such an outcome, I certainly would have done all in my power tae do so. I miss them both dearly each and every day since they passed."

"And what of Sabina?"

Killian stared at Sabina who was mayhap attending the festivities but hardly appeared as though she fit in. "I can only surmise if she has not taken her vows at the abbey by now, she may ask tae return here. I am not certain why the mother superior has allowed Sabina tae stay there so long without such a commitment. Mayhap Time has other plans for her as well. Ye will welcome her home if this is her choice?"

"You know I will. This is where she belongs. I never thought her joining a nunnery was a good choice for her. Everyone knew 'twas a mistake except my sister. But I could not gainsay her decision considering all she had been through." Amiria shuddered while she apparently relived the memory.

"Aye. Yer sister is a troubled soul. 'Twill take time tae heal such a wound."

"What of Aiden, Lynet, and Patrick?"

Killian chuckled. "What of them, Amiria? Lynet is happily married and raising her family with Ian in the north. Patrick continues tae foster with Laird de Deveraux and his countess, and he is also well. As for Aiden, he lost his inheritance when Dristan was given these lands. Yer brother seeks a name for himself. Surely ye wouldnae deny him finding his own destiny and a bonny wife tae call his own."

"Nay. I only want his happiness as well."

"Then, as ye can see, none of the lives around ye have changed that much no matter that Ella altered her own son's destiny."

Amiria squeezed his arm. "I suppose all worked out as it should," she said before whispering in his ear. "And you have a son..."

"...but Faramond must never know the kinship we share, other than I claim Conrad through my marriage tae his mother."

"I understand, Uncle," she murmured before continuing. "Do you suppose others from some future place in time will find their way to Berwyck?"

Killian's gaze swept the room before landing on Fletcher, Berwyck's captain of the guard and Lady Jenna who had shown up on the beach recently. He supposed their fate had already run its course in some transformed state of time. In his heart, he knew they, too, had found love. "I have no doubt Time isnae finished bringing these future gals tae yer shores, Amiria."

She gave another small sigh. "Dristan will not be pleased if he loses another of his friends to these women who keep disrupting our lives."

Silence swept over them as though they were both lost in thought about events they wished could have changed or had altered those living at Berwyck.

Before Killian formed a reply, Dristan came over to his wife and held out his hand. "You are looking far too melancholy, my lovely wife. This is a celebration. Come and dance with me before the children demand your attention... or would you prefer to get your sword and have a go at me outside to cheer you?"

Amiria laughed before she kissed Killian's cheek. Taking her husband's outstretched hand, she playfully swatted at him. "'Twould be a pleasure, my lord, to dance with you. We shall leave practicing with our swords for the morrow," she declared with a bright smile.

Dristan pulled his wife into his arms. Bending down, he kissed the top of her head. "You should go dance with your bride, Killian, before someone else decides to run off with her," he laughed with a smirk.

"No one would dare," Killian said with a frown while his gaze traveled to his wife dancing with one of Berwyck's guardsman."

Dristan chuckled once more. "I but jest with you, old man. Go to your wife while I take my fair lady for a turn about our hall. You have waited long enough to finally claim Lady Ella as your bride!"

Killian watched the pair leave before he grumbled about hardly being that old, not that there was anyone near to hear his words. Grabbing hold of his cup, he downed what remained of his ale before rising and lessening the distance to his wife.

He tapped Ulrick's shoulder before reaching for Ella's hand. "Find yerself a new partner," he ordered with a sly grin. "This lady is now taken."

The thump upon Killian's back would have felled a weaker man. "'Tis about time you got off your sorry arse to dance with your wife," Ulrick laughed before looking Killian up and down as though accessing his worth. "I suppose I shall be leaving the lady in good hands. 'T hath been a pleasure, my lady." He gave a short bow and left to find another to dance with.

Killian swept Ella into his arms but did not continue the dance. Her arms wound their way up and around his neck. Ella pressed herself lightly into his body and Killian stifled a groan as he felt a part of him stir to life. Her smile had him wishing they were alone in their room.

Ella began playing with his hair while they stood in the middle of the hall just slightly swaying to the music. "So...." she murmured in a low sultry tone. "Do you not wish to continue the dance?"

"If we must, although I do have other ideas in mind," he said, pulling her even closer 'til he heard her intake of breath. She could hardly mistake his meaning.

"Do you now?" Ella turned her head to look around the room. "I doubt they would miss us that much, not with a new keg of ale being brought up from the cellars to drink and the minstrels playing to keep them entertained."

"Do ye think so?" he asked. "What of the lord and lady of Berwyck?"

Ella laughed. "I am certain they would completely understand if we were to disappear to our chamber to continue our celebration in private."

"Then let us make a hasty exit so I can at last make you mine," he replied in a husky whisper. Taking her hand, he began leading his wife from the room and up the turret stairs 'til they found their chamber. As the door closed behind them, Killian slid the bolt into place.

Ella crossed the room to pour them wine. She held out the cup. "Would you like a drink?" she asked.

"Nay." He came to stand before her and took the chalice from her hands to place it upon the table. He was surprised to witness his hand actually shaking when he reached out to cup her cheek. She leaned into his palm and sighed.

"Then what do you want," she asked while she began tugging at his tunic.

"Only you," he murmured before he bent down to steal a kiss.

Hours later and with Ella curled up against his side, Killian could barely contain his joy of at last having this incredible woman as his wife. He pulled her closer while her fingers playfully ran over his chest.

"Ye have made me a happy man this day, wife," he murmured as he kissed the top of his head.

"We have waited long enough to claim one another," she said before leaning back to look into his eyes. "You do forgive me for putting you through all this torment for all these years?"

"There is nothing tae forgive. Ye only did what was necessary tae bring our separation tae an end. An end that I initiated so ye could save yer son. I cannae complain that, in this new altered life, ye have also given me a son. Ye are an incredible woman, my lady," he whispered, before he claimed her lips in a searing kiss.

"Just Ella," she said teasingly, when he at last let her take a breath.

Killian brushed his hand across her cheek. "Aye… at last ye are mine, Ella of Clan MacLaren. We have been blessed tae have made our way back tae one another and I plan on never leaving yer side again."

"I will hold you to your vow, husband," she said before she moved to lie on top of him. "Now love me again to seal your vow. I am done traveling through Time and have finally made my way home to you."

As Ella bent down to place her lips upon his own, Killian fulfilled the promise to his lady he made all those years ago in another life. He had promised her that love would find them no matter how much time would pass. *Time* may have been their enemy but Killian would now let Time quietly pass them by. He and Ella were now together. He would not ask anything more from Time than that...

Thank you so very much for purchasing a copy of **Love Will Find You**. I hope you enjoyed reading Killian and Ella's journey through Time as much as I had writing it. **Reviews** are the lifeblood of an Indie, self-pubished author like myself. I would sincerely appreciate it if you would take few moments to write a review at the retailer where you purchased the book, Goodreads, or BookBub. Even a few words that you enjoyed it will help. Thank you!

AUTHOR'S NOTE

How about a little history?

Berwyck Castle is the central hub for all my medieval and time travel stories (and has a cameo in my Regency's - A Family of Worth series). Early on, I told myself that the members of my MacLaren family/clan would always be grounded in the twelfth-century. One should never say never because while driving one day a major plot bunny invaded my head and the next thing I knew Killian of Clan MacLaren was in a time travel.

As noted in my other stories, Berwick-Upon-Tweed is the location I used in my debut novel, *If My Heart Could See You*, because it was right on the England/Scotland border. For whatever reasons, I changed the spelling to Berwyck in order to have free license to use the castle as I needed in order for the estate to fit my stories.

AUTHOR'S NOTE

You may be wondering how I chose the locations of where Ella would live and/or travel. Funny thing is, I think it was sheer luck. Google Earth has become my friend and made it relatively easy to find neighboring estates near or close enough to Warkworth Castle where I have Riorden and Katherine de Devereaux living. Katherine, as you recall, is like a daughter to Ella and she would have traveled to Warkworth whenever she was able.

Founded in the late twelfth century by the monks of Meaux Abbey, Wyke on Hull was later renamed Kings-town upon Hull in 1299. Hull became a market town, supply port, trading hub, and a way for the monks to export their wool. The abbey was closed in 1539 by King Henry VIII. It was demolished (much like the castle at Berwick-Upon-Tweed), and the stones were used to build defenses for the town of Kingston upon Hull. The site of the abbey is a Scheduled Ancient Monument.

As for Hull Castle, I may have tinkered with time just a little as the keep wasn't constructed by Henry VIII until 1542 to protect Hull from attack by France. Hence my reference to Faramond building a wall. The castle was constructed to defend the east side of town and to also ensure loyalty of the population. The castle was rectangular with brick and stone foundations and had two large curved bastions containing chambers on the west and east ends. The three story keep was located in the middle.

Hull seemed to fit my need to have Ella living on an estate near a waterway. Any references mentioned regarding the castle's infrastructure in *Love Will Find You* is fictitious on the part of this author.

AUTHOR'S NOTE

And this little bit of history would not be complete if I didn't mention Conisbrough Castle where Ella resides for a brief moment in time. This particular castle was a medieval fortification in South Yorkshire. It was initially built in the eleventh century by William de Warenne, the Earl of Surrey, after the Norman conquest of England in 1066. The castle remained in the family line into the fourteenth century, despite being seized several times by the Crown. The castle was made up of an inner and outer bailey, the former surrounded by a stone curtain wall defended by six fortified towers and the castle keep. Any reference to this being owned by Henry de Rune is completely fictitious on the part of this author.

ACKNOWLEDGMENTS

Dearest Reader:

I would first like to take this opportunity to thank you, my dearest reader, for purchasing a copy of this novel. I feel like *Love Will Find You* became a work of love and after such a long drought for a full-length story from me, I hope you feel it was worth the wait. I really enjoyed writing Killian and Ella's story and felt it was time to write something with an older couple. I figure if I'm still crying in all the right places after reading it multiple times, then I hope it will fill your heart with joy, too.

Congratulations goes out to Dee Foster! Dee won the auction to name a character in one of my books from the Buns & Roses fundraiser I attended in October 2019 in Dallas, Texas. You can thank Dee for "Isabel" who had more of a role than just one quick scene. Dee – I hope you like what I did with this character.

One never knows… she could just happen to have a story of her own one day.

Thank you to Caroline Warfield who took time out of her own writing schedule to beta read this story. I sincerely appreciate all your efforts on my behalf.

A huge thank you to Jude Knight who is my editor for this project. Jude spent hours ensuring that all the moving parts in this story worked. Yes, I wrote myself into a corner on this one, but Jude is the one who really made it shine. I couldn't have pulled this off without her. Thank you to the moon and back, Jude! You really are a Goddess among women!

Thank you to my daughter Jessica who continues to be my sounding board when things just don't click in a story. I don't know what I'd do without her to my run ideas by her even though I usually change things around in order for my voice to be heard. Thank you, Jessie.

Thanks to my mother who continues to patiently wait for another book to cry over. I love you, mom!

Thank you to my wonderful supporters in my Timeless Knights & Maiden's Facebook street team and also my public group, The Historical & Time Travel World of Sherry Ewing. All your efforts on my behalf to get the word out about my books don't go unnoticed. I sincerely appreciate all your support and your friendship.

Until the next time, I hope to have new material coming your way soon and I look forward to reading your posts on our mutual social media outlets.

With warm regards,
Sherry Ewing

OTHER BOOKS BY SHERRY EWING

Medieval & Time Travel Series

To Love A Scottish Laird: De Wolfe Pack Connected World

Sometimes you really can fall in love at first sight…

Lady Catherine de Wolfe knows she must find a husband before her brother chooses one for her. A tournament to celebrate the wedding of the Duke of Normandy might be her answer. She does not expect to fall for a man after just one touch. Laird Douglas MacLaren of Berwyck is invited to the tournament by the Duke of Normandy. He goes to ensure Berwyck's safety once Henry takes the throne. He does not expect to become entranced by a woman who bumps into him. Yet, nothing is ever quite that simple. Not everyone is happy with the union of this English lady and a Scottish laird. From the shores of France, to Berwyck Castle on the border between their countries, Douglas and Catherine must find their way to protect their newfound love.

To Love An English Knight: De Wolfe Pack Connected World

Can a chance encounter lead to love?

Sir Charles de Grey is in turmoil. He cannot forget the Scottish lass he kissed in Caen, but her jealous spite toward the lady he was sworn to guard infuriated him. Living at Berwyck Castle, he is torn between his desire for Lady Freya and his need to rebuke her sometimes reckless behavior. Leaving her almost tears him apart, but it might give him time to recover some balance.

Lady Freya of Clan MacLaren didn't expect to become blinded by love until she became quickly besotted on first seeing the English knight in Caen. How quickly everything fell apart when she defies him! Even worse, when he begins to show signs of returning her feelings, he receives a message from home that will tear them apart. Defying him again may put an end to any chance they may have together, but what other choice does she have when he leaves her?

Can the fragile love they found blossom into something more or will circumstances beyond their control continue to provoke behavior that keeps them apart?

If My Heart Could See You: The MacLaren's, A Medieval Romance (Book One)

When you're enemies, does love have a fighting chance? Amiria of Berwyck vows to protect her people by pledging her oath of fealty to the very enemy who has laid siege to her home. Dristan, the Devil's Dragon of Blackmore, has a reputation to uphold as champion knight of his king. Lies, treachery, and deceit attempt to tear them apart, but only love will bring them together

For All of Ever: The Knights of Berwyck, A Quest Through Time (Book One)

Sometimes to find your future, you must look to the past... Katherine dreamed of her knight all her life yet how could she know she'd be thrown back into the past? Nothing prepares Riorden for the beautiful vision of a strangely clad ghost appearing in his chamber. Centuries keep them apart but will Time give them a chance at finding love?

Only For You: The Knights of Berwyck, A Quest Through Time (Book Two)

Sometimes it's hard to remember that true love conquers all, only after the battle is over... Katherine has it all but settling into her duties at Warkworth is dangerous to her well-being. Consumed with memories of his father, Riorden must deal with his sire's widow. Torn apart, Time becomes their enemy while Marguerite continues her ploy to keep Riorden at her side. With all hope lost, will Katherine & Riorden find a way to save their marriage?

Hearts Across Time: The Knights of Berwyck (Books One & Two)

Sometimes all you need is to just believe… Hearts Across Time is a special edition box set that combines Katherine and Riorden's stories together from *For All of Ever* and *Only For You.*

A Knight To Call My Own: The MacLaren's, A Medieval Romance (Book Two)

When your heart is broken, is love still worth the risk? Lynet of Clan MacLaren knows how it feels to love someone and not have that love returned. Ian MacGillivray has returned to Berwyck in search of a bride. Who will claim the fair Lynet? The price will be high to ensure her safety and even higher to win her love.

To Follow My Heart: The Knights of Berwyck, A Quest Through Time (Book Three)

Love is a leap. Sometimes you need to jump… Jenna Sinclair is dealing with a horrendous break up with her fiancé when she finds herself pulled through time to twelfth century England. Fletcher Monroe has spent too much time pining away for a woman who will never be his until a strangely clad woman magically appears. Torn between the past and the present, will their growing love survive a journey through Time?

The Piper's Lady in Never Too Late, A Bluestocking Belles Collection 2017

True love binds them. Deceit divides them. Will they choose love? Lady Coira Norwood spent her youth traveling with her grandfather.

Now well past the age men prefer when they choose a wife, she has resigned herself to remain a maiden. But everything changes once she arrives at Berwyck Castle. She cannot resist a dashing knight who runs to her rescue, but would he give her a second look?

Garrick of Clan MacLaren can hold his own with the trained Knights of Berwyck, but as the clan's piper they would rather he play his instruments to entertain them—or lead them into battle—than to fight with a sword upon the lists. Only when he sees a lady across the training field and his heart sings for the first time does he begin to wish to be something he is not.

Will a simple misunderstanding between them threaten what they have found in one another or will they at last let love into their hearts?

Love Will Find You: The Knights of Berwyck, A Quest Through Time (Book Four)

Sometimes a moment is all we have…

Ella Fitzpatrick is a woman with a secret. As she comes and goes from Berwyck Castle, seeking refuge within its gates, she yearns to be reunited with the one for whom she crossed time from the twenty-first century. She has lived another lifetime in the twelfth century waiting for the date of their reunion and it is almost upon her. But how could she have known the man she believes she loves is not the person she needs?

Killian of Clan MacLaren has been infatuated with Ella for many a year but has guarded his heart, knowing her affection lies with another. When Ella must flee Berwyck, Killian vows to escort her to her encounter with destiny. But passion flares between them and there is no doubt the bond they have is far greater than either of them expected.

Their time together is running out. Killian has a decision to make that might give him and Ella a future together. If you could change someone's past, would you seize the moment?

One Last Kiss: The Knights of Berwyck, A Quest Through Time (Book Five)

Sometimes it takes a miracle to find your heart's desire…

Scotland, 1182: Banished from his homeland, Thomas of Clan Kincaid lives among distant relatives, reluctantly accepting he may never return home… until the castle's healer tells him of a woman traveling across time…

Dare he believe the impossible?

Present Day, Michigan: Jade Calloway is used to being alone, and as Christmas approaches, she's skeptical when told she'll embark on an extraordinary journey. But when a ring magically appears, and she sees a ghostly man in her dreams...

Dare she believe in the possible?

Regency's

A Kiss For Charity: A de Courtenay Novella (Book One)

Love heals all wounds but will their pride keep them apart?

Young widow, Grace, Lady de Courtenay, has no idea how a close encounter with a rake at a masquerade ball would make her yearn for love again. Lord Nicholas Lacey is captivated by a lovely young woman he encounters at a masquerade. Considering the company she keeps, she might be interested in becoming his mistress. From the darkened paths of Vauxhall Gardens to a countryside estate called Hollystone Hall, Nicholas and Grace must set aside their differences in order to let love into their hearts.

The Earl Takes A Wife: A de Courtenay Novella (Book Two)

It began with a memory, etched in the heart.

Lady Celia Lacey is too young for a husband, especially man-about-town Lord Adrian de Courtenay. But when she meets him at a house party, she falls in love.

Adrian finds the appealing innocent impossible to forget, though she is barely out of the schoolroom and a relative by marriage.

His sister's deception brings them together, but destroys their happiness. Can they reach past the hurt to the love that still burns?

Nothing But Time: A Family of Worth (Book One)

They will risk everything for their forbidden love…

When Lady Gwendolyn Marie Worthington is forced to marry a man old enough to be her father, she concludes love will never enter her life. Her husband is a cruel man who blames her for his own failings. Then she meets her brother's attractive business associate, and all those longings she had thought gone forever suddenly reappear.

A long-term romance holds no appeal for Neville Quinn, Earl of Drayton until an unexpected encounter with the sister of the Duke of Hartford. Still, he resists giving his heart to another woman, especially one who belongs to another man.

Chance encounters lead to intimate dinners, until Neville and Gwendolyn flee to Berwyck Castle at Scotland's border hoping beyond reason their fragile love will survive the vindictive reach of Gwendolyn's possessive husband. Before their journey is over, Gwendolyn will risk losing the only love she has ever known.

One Moment In Time: A Family of Worth (Book Two)

One moment in time may be enough, if it lasts forever…

When the man Lady Roselyn Anne Winslow has loved since she was a young girl begins to court her, Roselyn thinks all her dreams have come true… until the dream turns into a nightmare.

Lady Roselyn is everything Edmond Worthington, 9th Duke of

Hartford, could ask for in a wife and he is delighted to find she returns his love… until he loses her, not once but twice.

From England's ballrooms, to Berwyck Castle and a tropical island that is anything but paradise, Edmond and Roselyn face ruthless enemies who will do anything to tear them apart. Can they recover their one moment in time?

Under the Mistletoe

A new suitor seeks her hand. An old flame holds her heart. Which one will she meet under the kissing bough? When Margaret Templeton is requested to act as hostess at a Christmas party she did not think she would see the man who once held her heart. Frederick Maddock, Viscount Beacham never forgot the young woman he had fallen in love with. Will the two finally put down their differences and once again fall in love?

A Second Chance At Love in
Fire & Frost: A Bluestocking Belles Collection

Can the bittersweet frost of lost love be rekindled into a burning flame?

Viscount Digby Osgood returns to London after a two-year absence, planning to avoid the woman he courted and then left. Surely she has moved on with her life; even married by now. A bit of encouragement from a friend, however, pushes him to seek the lady out. Can she ever forgiven him and give them a second chance at love?

Lady Constance Whittles has only cared for one man in her life. Even after he broke her heart, it remains fixed on him. Another man tries to replace him, but she soon learns she can never feel for him a shadow of what she still feels for Digby. One brief encounter with Digby confirms it; she is more than willing to forgive him. Can they truly take up where they left off?

Charity projects and a Frost Fair on the Thames bring them together, but another stands in their way. Will he tear them apart?

You can find out more about Sherry's work on her website at www.SherryEwing.com and at online retailers.

SOCIAL MEDIA

Website: www.SherryEwing.com
Email: Sherry@SherryEwing.com
Bluestocking Belles: www.bluestockingbelles.net/
Amazon Author Page: http://amzn.to/1TrWtoy
Bookbub: www.bookbub.com/authors/sherry-ewing
Facebook: www.Facebook.com/SherryEwingAuthor
Goodreads: www.Goodreads.com/author/show/8382315.Sherry_Ewing
Instagram: https://instagram.com/sherry.ewing
Pinterest: www.Pinterest.com/SherryLEwing
Tumblr: https://sherryewing.tumblr.com
Twitter: www.Twitter.com/Sherry_Ewing
YouTube: http://www.youtube.com/SherryEwingauthor

Sign Me Up!
Newsletter: http://bit.ly/2vGrqQM
Facebook Street Team:
www.facebook.com/groups/799623313455472/
Facebook Official Fan page: https://www.facebook.com/groups/356905935241836/

ABOUT SHERRY EWING

Sherry Ewing picked up her first historical romance when she was a teenager and has been hooked ever since. A bestselling author, she writes historical and time travel romances to awaken the soul one heart at a time. When not writing, she can be found in the San Francisco area at her day job as an Information Technology Specialist.

Learn more about Sherry at:
Website: www.SherryEwing.com
Email: Sherry@SherryEwing.com

Made in United States
Orlando, FL
21 January 2024